J—, BLACK BAM AND THE MASQUERADERS

ALSO BY GARTH ST OMER

"Syrop" in *Introduction Two: Stories by New Writers*
A Room on the Hill
Shades of Grey
Nor Any Country
Prisnms

GARTH ST OMER

J—, BLACK BAM AND THE MASQUERADERS

INTRODUCTION: JEREMY POYNTING

PEEPAL TREE

First published by Faber and Faber
in Great Britain in 1972
This new edition published in 2016 by
Peepal Tree Press Ltd
17 King's Avenue
Leeds LS6 1QS
England

ISBN13: 9781845232436

Supported by
ARTS COUNCIL
ENGLAND

For Gallion

"All in compassion ends
so differently from what the heart arranged"
— Derek Walcott

LETTING THE CAT OUT OF THE BAG: TRUTH AND LIES IN *J—, BLACK BAM AND THE MASQUERADERS*

JEREMY POYNTING

Garth St Omer's fourth novel is the coping stone in a sequence that includes *The Lights on the Hill* (1968) (in *Shades of Grey*) and *Nor Any Country* (1969), focusing on the lives of the Breville brothers, Paul and Peter. Little happens in this novel that has not been signalled in the previous two, but the excavation of the why and the how make it perhaps the most absorbing of the series. Readers of *Nor Any Country* know that Peter Breville returns to his native island (St Lucia) after eight years away, latterly in England, reunites with his abandoned wife, Phyllis, and takes her and his nephew Michael with him when he goes to work as a lecturer at the university in the larger island to the north (Jamaica). Readers of *The Lights on the Hill*, set on the university campus, know that Breville has reputedly been engaging in an extramarital affair, drinking heavily and is seen by the two central characters, Stephenson and Thea (who reappear briefly in this novel) in a fight with Phyllis in the university grounds (an incident replayed in this novel). What may surprise the reader of the two previous books is that there is a period of harmony before the descent into discord.

Readers of *Nor Any Country* also know that Paul Breville, Peter's elder brother, initially the most promising of the two, has remained in St Lucia having fallen from grace after getting his girlfriend pregnant and refusing to marry her; we know that he has been sacked from his school post and has refused offers of civil service positions that he regards as below his dignity. On his return, Peter finds his brother exhibiting signs of madness – either, as Paul claims, an antic mask to distract public gaze away

7

from his private inner conflicts, or an actual breakdown resulting from his feelings of entrapment within the narrow, Catholic-dominated colonial society of 1950s St Lucia.

J—, Black Bam and the Masqueraders has a thematic unity and fictive coherence that make it rewarding if read on its own, but, as argued in the introductions to the earlier books, there is much to be gained by reading the three books as narratives in dialogue with each other.

Dialogue is embedded in the structure of *J—, Black Bam and the Masqueraders* itself, as a montage of two intercutting narratives: a third person account of Peter's and Phyllis's marriage and his affair with Jeannine; and Paul Breville's first person epistolary account, addressed to Peter, that expands on the facts known to Peter about his social "disgrace". The fact that the letters are addressed to Peter but Paul is doubtful that he will ever send them suggests a subtext. The letters are unfailingly generous and apologetic in their references to Peter, but silent or ambivalent around Peter's and Phyllis's marriage and its motivation. Paul, after all, has been witness both to its beginnings and the puzzling ease with which it is resumed on Peter's return.

Peter, as portrayed in Paul's narrative, clearly believes that he has escaped from the influences of family, school and church as institutional expressions of the dominant ideologies of race and class in St Lucia. However, Paul's meticulous revisiting of their shaping influences in his life points to the absence of a similar honest reflection on Peter's part. We may well conclude both that Peter's escape from the past is not as complete as he imagines and that this has a great deal to do with his reluctance to look within.

The novel begins with Paul, writing some two years after Peter's visit, and following the death of their mother and the shattering of their father's life by a stroke. Paul's account, from his youth to just before Peter's return to the island, has two rhythms: a mostly linear narrative of events, and a helical pattern of analysis, which sometimes returns to earlier incidents with greater under-standing. The narrative dealing with Peter and Phyllis is divided into three non-sequential sections: the first begins some two years after their arrival in Jamaica when Peter's affair with Jeannine is central to his battles with Phyllis (pp. 34-48); the second episode, which returns to the beginning of their time in Jamaica (pp. 83-98), tracks, after a year of relative contentment, Peter's path away from Phyllis to the point where he begins his affair; and the third part (pp. 106-114, 126-131), documents Peter's increasing engagement with their child and Phyllis's fight back and revenge on Jeannine. St Omer is generally a reluctant user of an authorial voice that is external to his characters, but in the second part it is used extensively, recording the limitations of Peter's self-perception.

As in St Omer's previous novels (the early novella *Syrop* is quite different in artistic vision and style), there is an intensive focus on character within the context of family life and close relationships. Little need be said here about the empathetic but clearsighted portrayal of how a marriage falls apart, except to note that the seriousness with which St Omer treats the domestic has remained rare in Caribbean fiction, at least until the point at which women novelists emerged to expand its attention to the inwardness of lives. It is also worth noting St Omer's honesty in his treatment of the misogyny that bedevils the relationships between many of his men with women, and his acute, historically-informed sense of the social and cultural forms this takes. In the episodes dealing with Peter and Phyllis we see misogyny in action. In Paul's painful admissions of male cruelty (pp. 99-105, 115-125) we see an analysis how the power relations of class, culture and race impact on his treatment of his girlfriend Patsy, though he never quite sees the cultural constructions of gender that shape his behaviour. This is St Omer's scrupulous realism: that whilst the reader can see this clearly, his character does not – in a way that is consistent with the kinds of discourse Paul has access to in St Lucia in the early and mid 1950s.

What the introduction will suggest is how the domestic speaks to wider contexts, though the novel says little explicitly about its characters' location in history, society and politics. But through an intensive focus on individuals St Omer makes a critique of the role of the intellectual middle class the politics of decolonisation that connects to the work of George Lamming (particularly *Of Age and Innocence* (1958) and Orlando Patterson's *An Absence of Ruins* (1967). All St Omer's novels are acutely observant of the dynamics of class, culture and colour as experienced in individual lives, but none is so emphatically Fanonian as *J—, Black Bam*, none as insistent on the psychological violence inflicted and then self-inflicted on black and brown West Indians because of the failure to confront the inherited mentalities of the slave and colonial past.

As in St Omer's previous novels, images and themes that exist on the edge of earlier narratives move to the centre of this one. The trope of masquerading is one of these. The theme has a significant but perhaps additive role at the end of *A Room on the Hill*, where the competing processions of Old Alphonse, carnival masqueraders and Anne-Marie's funeral procession clash in the streets. In *Shades of Grey*, the processions are mostly of a solemnly religious kind, but in *Nor Any Country*, the figure of Julien the fisherman in the Devil mask both fascinates and terrifies Peter as a child – and returns to him in a dream in this novel. Here, the descriptions of masquerading are more extensive and its psychological and socio-historical significance is explored in ways that connect to a wider discourse in African American and Caribbean writing. At one level masking is concerned with acts of conscious or unwitting disguise, such as in Paul Laurence Dunbar's famous lyric of 1896, "We wear the mask that grins and lies/ it hides our cheeks and shields our eyes –",[1] a shield from observation, such as Paul's claim that he is playing mad to hide his pain. It may also be a pathology of shame, as Fanon explores in his early work on Martinique, *Black Skins, White Masks* (1952);[2] here Paul's confessions of inadequacy and need for white approval provide a moving case study. But the act of masking has other resonances, as a ritual performance of resistance and subversion, as in Trinidad carnival (qv. Earl Lovelace's later novel, *The Dragon Can't Dance* (1979)) and Jamaican Jonkonnu, elements of which may include the mocking of the high by the low or the acting out of desires that polite society insists be hidden. And as Sylvia Wynter's seminal essay, "Jonkonnu in Jamaica: Towards the interpretation of Folk Dance as a Cultural Process" documents,[3] Caribbean masking has its origins in West African rituals, when, for instance, men take on the roles of Gods. As such it challenges the Euro-creole norms that have dominated Caribbean cultural life. Paul's responses to two street performances of masquerade, observed at different stages in his life, lead in the first instance to an act of betrayal and racial self-contempt, in the second to a moment of revelation.

Running through his treatment of the trope of the mask is St Omer's concern with the ethics of truthfulness and the consequences of its absence. This is the moral centre of this novel, but one that St Omer leaves the reader to deduce. His is not the voice of the preacher/prophet standing on the moral high ground.

The cultural location and historical origins of the masquerades that Paul witnesses on the street (about which St Omer resists authorial explication) also provide the novel with a more organic route into reflections on the historical shaping of the present than are made in the earlier novels. In *J–, Black Bam* there are several episodes that reflect on the continuing reverberations of the organisation and culture of slave society in the shaping of the mentalities and behaviours of the present. These include the gap between the sexual and cultural expression of the "unrespectable" black masses, and the buttoned-up repressions of the respectable middle class. Thus, the social make-up of the eponymous masquerade group that Paul witnesses (pp. 121-124) condenses the racial and cultural crisis he confronts. Like Paul, the two leading masquerade figures are black. There is J—, leader of the group, whose abbreviated name,[4] whose frayed black suit and "not-so-white shirt" and his "solemn pompous dignity" signals a man who has fallen from the middle, or at least educated classes, and is now burlesquing their pretensions. At the other pole is Black Bam, the dissolute drunkard whose racial and class identity is embedded in his name, who plays the role of the "vicious cow", pretending to break free from the restraining ropes of the other masqueraders – an enactment of social threat.[5]

Structurally, in the novel, Paul's second witnessing of a masquerade performance prompts his own turn towards disguise (the mask of madness) but also his own act of self-revelation through the letters to Peter – letting his cat out of the bag, so to speak. One element in the masqueraders' performance is the demand for money (*"Quatre sous pour 'oir-le."*) from the watching crowd so that the hooded masquerader (Black Bam) is exposed to view, to the cry of *"Chat en fouga"*, cat in the bag. This and the earlier performance of street masquerade that Paul recalls (where his

11

response veers between pleasure, embarrassment and angry rejection) connect to the tensions he experiences in the act of writing. In "examination and evaluation" he finds "an orderliness [...] control over what I write about events which once overwhelmed me" (pp. 29-30)). but he also dreads "the times when everything seems to rush out of my memory. I am unable to cope with the outpouring" – an image that is libidinal and orgasmic, pointing to the continuing power of the desires that have motivated his behaviour.

As suggested above, the emotional core of the novel lies in the contrasting voices of the two brothers, and here St Omer challenges the reader's expectations of the two modes of telling. How are we to respond to Paul's first person narrative, the story of someone who is seen by others as deranged and who has been explicit about the performative, masking aspects of his behaviour? On most scores, Paul has the features of an unreliable narrator, a character who is, on the surface, calculatedly unattractive. He is ungracious, obsessional, repressed, rule-bound, and inaccessible to other characters. He has rejected his pregnant girlfriend, Patsy, and refused to take responsibility for their son, Michael, even after Patsy's suicide. Peter by contrast is open, evidently engaging and sought-after by others, and liberal/progressive in his politics whereas Paul has been self-confessedly reactionary. Peter has "adopted" Michael and brought him with Phyllis to Jamaica (though Michael plays no role in the novel – and we may wonder how he may be responding to the warfare between Peter and Phyllis). Paul is presented through his own eyes and voice, whereas the picture we have of Peter comes mainly through the perceptions of others, principally Paul, Jeannine and Phyllis. Only towards the end of the novel, when Peter stares at his wasted face in a mirror, do we see the beginnings of self-reflection. By the end of the novel, St Omer has turned our expectations of these two modes of telling on their heads. We are likely to conclude that Paul's narrative is characterised by honesty and truth, whereas, again and again, the reader is drawn to the conclusion that there is a conspiracy of misperception between Peter and those from whom he receives some reflection of his being in the world. It is the reader who is invited to perceive the gap between the open, honest face Peter offers to the world and the hollow, self-deceiving man who stares back at himself through the mirror.

As in *Shades of Grey*, St Omer uses one narrative to throw light on the other. Between the brothers' stories, there is not just a shared family past, but tropes that move between the two narratives, such as those concerned with the angles and locations of perception. In Paul's narrative there is an explicit gap between how he perceives his behaviour "now", as he writes, and how he saw it as he performed/experienced it. But even he, thankfully for the reader's interpretive engagement with his character, is not always shown to be aware of the metaphorical threads that run through the narrative he tells. The two dominant tropes of perception are those of verticality and distance, where Paul frequently describes situations where he is either looking up or looking down on the observed scene, or where he imagines himself being looked up to or down upon. It is a trope that points both to Paul's habitual way of seeing and to the hierarchical constructs of the island society in which he has become entrapped. Distance from and feeling external to what he is observing is the other constant. In a parallel way, one of the striking tropes used to describe the relationship between Peter and his white mistress, Jeannine, focuses on the angle of view from which she prefers to look at him, how she "turned away from the contradictions of his open face – from the nose that was flat, the forehead too broad and bulging, the eyes that were both dead and piercing. She preferred the single, uncomplicated line of his face in profile" (p. 35). This may suggest Jeannine's particular reluctance to perceive the Africanness of Peter's features, but it also points to a more general failure to look at things directly and as they are, one of the key themes in this third person narrative. It also connects the contradictions embedded in Peter himself to the processes of perception, with eyes that see (piercing) and don't see (dead), to Peter's sharpness when he looks outwards, but reluctance to look within.

Paul's confessional narrative is often shocking in its revelations of callousness towards Patsy, but we begin to believe in him as a character who is unremittingly honest and increasingly percep-

13

tive about the roots of his behaviour and his responsibility for it. With Peter, the reader is left to "read" the spaces, challenged to make an analysis of the relationship between what Peter says and what Peter does and what other characters say about him. The unavoidable conclusion is that whereas the "closed" Paul is openly honest, the "open" Peter lives a life of constant self-deception that damages both himself and those around him, and that the contradictions point to a dangerously empty space within him – and by implication in the social milieu to which he belongs. So, in this study of the ethics of honesty, we have one character who is regarded as mad by those around him, and another who, whatever his marital misdemeanours, is treated as sane. But if sanity is at some level marked by the truthfulness of perceptions to a shared reality, St Omer invites us to question which of the brothers is actually mad, which sane.

Whilst St Omer's portrayals of character are too rooted in the distinctive features of the fictive personal and family biography he gives them to permit casual reading of them as representative types, the way he presents what Peter says about the late 1950s Caribbean world and the responsibility of the "intellectual" in it suggests that these are much repeated performances that probably don't wholly originate from his own thought processes, but are the collective mantras of the wider (university) intellectual middle class. We don't see much of these people, but we hear them in his voice.

It is through the interplay between individual psychological predispositions and the way the individual both makes sense of and is shaped by circumstance that St Omer offers his implied social and political vision. Thus, both in Paul's narrative and in Peter's memories (explored in *Nor Any Country*), the distinction is made between Paul's obsessional desire for success and Peter's more relaxed and casual attitudes to achievement. Both attitudes point to what are the public forums for the judgement of performance on the island. The starting point for Paul's self-analysis is his recognition of the obsessional in his behaviour, with the memory of a trivial old boy's race and his need to win ("ran as for my life"), and his "terror" that he won't win. This is confirmed by Peter's images of Paul in *Nor Any Country* – the excessive training,

14

his interminable hitting of a cricket ball in their yard. As Paul writes: "You alone knew how hard I worked for the admiration I pretended I did not care for. Your father assumed that my intense practising in the yard was normal. You knew it was abnormal and an exaggeration" (p. 72). The key phrase is "worked for the admiration", for it is Paul's analysis of *who* he seeks admiration from (or pretends he doesn't) that makes him realise how deeply embedded in a colonised structure of perception he has been and how this has shattered the integrity of his psyche. Here St Omer is at his most Fanonian, agreeing with the analysis of *Black Skin, White Masks* that living under the colonial master's actual or imagined gaze has several dimensions: in shaping how the colonised subject *thinks* the master sees him; in shaping his desire to perform in ways that elicit that other's approval – to the denial of himself – and in perverting the way he sees his "own people" by way of how he thinks the colonialist sees them.

As a child, Paul recalls pretending to be a white priest swinging the censer, or the old white man who drives by in his car ("My stern, authoritative silence, I hoped, was exactly like that of the old white man I had so carefully observed" (p. 50)). Only much later does he recognise the absurdity of this respect, when he learns that this man has a son who, in Paul's father's words, "has no damn ambition", but who, though a wastrel, is a man his father "would have removed his warder's cap to speak to" (p. 51). This seeding of self-contempt finds ready reinforcement in the church: "I beat my breast and repeated phrases about my unworthiness, no one yearned more achingly than I to become worthy" (p. 53). It is a religious sentiment, but it elides easily into Paul's attitudes towards his racial/cultural self. From Paul's descriptions of church-going (pp. 59-61) it is clear that at this time the church was a microcosm of the island's hierarchies of class and colour. It is why Paul refuses to have anything to do with the steelband that Peter leads, why he recalls standing *outside* the Methodist school building listening to members of the Art Society (the brown middle class, teachers, civil servants, clerks) performing European songs. "And yet I knew they were failures, despite their costumes and their performances… They were not professionals – not doctors nor lawyers – and they were not white" (p. 56). Paul has wanted to be the man *looking down* from the verandas of the white/brown elite's houses in the square, and if he can't be there, if he has to be seen in the street, he must show himself worthy of their admiration by his ostentatious separation from the disorderly rabble. ("I felt reassured and vindicated, as if my dissociation from you [Peter is leading a carnival procession] had become tangible for those on their verandas to hold" (p. 57)). The growing presence of the brown middle class in Columbus Square, living as if they were white, intensifies his desire to belong to that world, whilst reinforcing his sense that he is not really worthy of it: "I had also seen those others whose brown skins [...] had intimidated me no less than the white skins of their neighbours" (p. 59). (It is an observation that comments implicitly on Peter's youthful attraction to Phyllis, the daughter, albeit illegitimate, of a white planter, who in appearance only, belongs to that brown, mulatto class – even though Peter wants to be seen as rejecting the island's hierarchies of culture and skin.) Everything Paul experiences impresses on him the need for separation from the mass of black people – in church, in the streets – and it feeds his resentment of those who are black like him but who attempt to challenge the natural order, the absolute authority, for instance, of the white priests. There's the scandal of a black man striking a white priest, and Paul admits how he shared the self-contempt revealed in his mother's phrase when she is brought this story: "She repeated the words *vieux negre* many times, with exasperation and with disdain" (p. 61). Later, however, as he recalls the incident, Paul is able to enjoy the irony of the neighbour who claims she would offer her arse to the priest to kick as an even more humble variant of turning the other cheek.

Paul's colonised way of seeing is most brutally revealed in his confessions regarding Patsy. If his behaviour on the streets is comically absurd, his treatment of Patsy is tragically Fanonian. His narrative of the most shaming episode begins with his return from a cricket tour where he feels that his skill has been admired in ways that make his blackness irrelevant, though in retrospect he sees how racial self-contempt has poisoned his self-perception. There is the photograph where he recalls wanting to borrow a sweater from a rich friend, and being desperately anxious to wipe the sweat from "my black greasy forehead". Back at home, the gap between his desires and his racial status becomes painfully clear again, and he confesses that he "reached for her [Patsy] out of my renewed ordinariness[…] to vent my frustration and anger upon" (p. 71). Her defencelessness attracts him – lets him act out the role of the slave master with the cynical power to satisfy his lust and then drop her, as he believes, without consequence: "She did not threaten me. I feared no rebuff from her". His cruelty begins in his perceptions of Patsy that mingle desire ("I became erect again") and contempt: "Her new dress seemed too colourful, her lips too red, the stockings she wore pretentious. But her firm, well-shaped body invited me" though he is repelled by "her too-greased, half-Indian, half-Negroid hair" (p. 76).

His attraction to and contempt for Patsy is connected to the trope of masquerade. He recalls observing a group of masqueraders when "The flute music was as agile as monkeys. The drumming was a writhing, furious background […] The dancers' gyrations assumed a frenzy that even I found hypnotic" (p. 77). Despite himself he is drawn in, but then a novice dancer begins his artless performance, cruelly seduced to perform by Paul's mocking father. The analogies with sexual abandon are clear: "He leaped into the air, opened his legs, spread his arms… he shook his entire body as if he suffered an extraordinary fit. His exaggerated performance was ungraceful and inelegant" (p. 77). The connection with Patsy is there in Paul's response to the novice dancer and what follows: "The spell cast by the intensely beautiful dancing of the other masqueraders was broken. I turned and walked disgustedly away" (p. 78). He then encounters Patsy, is immediately sexually excited again and tells her to follow him to the beach. When she does:

> My mood, made up of irritation and disgust, was now enhanced by a feeling of power. The promptness of Patricia's response had helped to define that power for me […] I began to have again, but without the elation, the feeling of confidence I had had earlier. I was superior to the masqueraders, to those who watched them perform, to the drunkards before the rum-shops. (p. 80)

On the beach, having already decided to end their relationship, he penetrates her crudely and briefly, and dismisses her whilst still inside her. He has made her strip ("I could see she was amazed, possibly frightened… I could sense her uneasiness which, however, did not bother me" (p. 81). He knows she will not resist him because he has already silenced her by making "fun of her pronunciation and the patois expressions she transliterated when she tried to speak to me in English […] I knew that I deserved more than that pink umbrella and the too-oiled hair" (p. 80).

It is a rape using class and culture as weapons – and written with a merciless and effective economy. But the consequences – the almost simultaneous news that he has topped his class and that Patsy is pregnant – swiftly remind Paul that though he can behave like a slavemaster, he doesn't have his power, as his dismissal from his school post proves.

In Paul's self-confessions there is the implication that Peter has followed a different path, has evaded becoming his father's son, as Paul recognises he has internalised his father's voice. He confesses: "I did not realize that I was being to you [Peter] what your father had been to us" (p. 73). He recognises that his father's invention of a self has been based on fantasy and deceit. His assumption of a white cultural mask would be mocked as incompetent mimicry by that elite, whilst the common people he seeks to impress, he deeply despises. Paul sees that his mission has been even more self-damaging since it is both more deeply internalised and more achievable: "Mine was no longer make-believe. Its reality was less for others to see than for me to possess. I wished to give the impression that I was a superior being endowed naturally with genius and with talent" (p. 54).

Peter, by contrast, has rejected his father and the clutches of the church. In his youth he leads a carnival band and rubs shoulders with the street people that Paul and his father despise.[6] He also gets away from the island and achieves the education and status that Paul's fall from grace prevents him from realising. But what the brothers have in common, of course, is the painful consequences of getting a young woman pregnant at a crucial state of their careers. In the silences and distortions of Peter's representation of his relationship with Phyllis, in the deceits and hypocrisies of his behaviour, we see how much he, too, has been shaped by his past, and how reluctant he is to reflect on it. But whilst Phyllis and Patsy both belong socially, culturally and educationally to the mass of the unlettered, there is a crucial difference: Phyllis is light-skinned with long straight hair, and it becomes clear that, in his youth, Peter was glamoured by the idea of possessing her, though he feels trapped into marriage by her pregnancy and rapidly discovers the difficulties of relationship to a woman who does not share his education.

These inclinations were seen in *Nor Any Country* in Peter's attraction, in London, first to Anna, the upper-class, opera-going black girl who straightens her hair and won't be seen in black immigrant neighbourhoods, and then to Daphne, a middle-class white woman. In this novel, the pattern is repeated in his relationship with Jeannine, white and part French. In a relationship lubricated by alcohol and Jeannine's admiration for his sexual inexhaustibility, whilst Peter regularly speaks about "man's inhumanity to man, about racism, exploitation, and greed", it is evident that Jeannine is unashamedly a member of that exploiting class and shares its values, as is evident in her complacent talk about Marcel and his island, new house and private beach and his cynically selfish expropriation of the previous peasant owners. If Peter does wonder briefly about the expropriated peasant, there is no evidence that he sees the contradictions in their relationship or recognises the repeated pattern of his glamouring by whiteness and wealth.

The consistency of Peter's unacknowledged attitudes is signalled in the scene (pp. 34-35) where he is lying in bed with Jeannine, listening to a concerto he recognises. Readers of *Nor Any Country* will know this is the Brandenburg Concerto, because it takes Peter back to "a room in London and tea and cake with Anna" (p. 35). Significantly it doesn't take him back to his other memory of listening to this music in the room of a rich, self-made black businessman (Keith Austin – also in *Nor Any Country*), where the image moves in the opposite direction – to a memory of a black woman in a state of trance playing a bamboo flute in a masquerade band. That, we might think, is the image that Peter, as man-of-the-people, should remember, but he doesn't.

The gap between what Peter says and does requires little comment, though we should note that St Omer suggests that he moves from a position of genuine feeling and critical thought to tired and meaningless repetition. We know his political statements have become habitual formulas by the dialogue tags St Omer uses ("he repeated", "he used to say"). We know how he is treating Phyllis even as he is talking (whilst lying in bed with Jeannine) about how "Man would never be happy... until he became responsible, not to a god or an idea but to himself and to his fellowman. Responsibility was what education must be about" (p. 35). There are indeed "Shadow Politics and the Shadow Religions" and truth in what Peter argues about the failure to remake the world after the end of slavery, but the failure to examine is as much his as it is of the political class he excoriates, and we never sense that the "we" he uses really means "I" as well:

> He had spoken of the Shadow Politics and the Shadow Religions – all unexamined, none understood, that separated and divided, and sapped strength that might have been collective. And he had sneered at independence *as it seemed the leaders of the islands understood it*. Independence, he maintained, no more than Emancipation, had been achievement. The slaves had not acquired one nor the island governments the other. But they had made of another's expedient concession their own achievement and were proud of it.
> "We are like children," *he used to say*, "mindlessly imitating adults, informing our fantasy with total and high seriousness... We are so busy imitating others that we have no time to do anything of our own" (p. 36) [my italics]

This is not the kind of speech Paul would or could have made, but it is evident from his letters that Paul has recognised how much the shadow politics of race and the shadow religion of self-contempt have shaped his mentality and behaviour, in a way that Peter, the rebel steelband leader with his wharf-rat friends has failed to recognise.

The problem for Peter is that whilst Jeannine is aware of his contradictions, she won't speak about them; she prefers to think of him as "vulnerable" rather than confront the "stories related on campus by staff and students alike, of his extreme brutality towards Phyllis" (p. 35). Phyllis is the one person who speaks truth to Peter, but though she makes accusations he cannot deny ("you leave me like a dog, and go to your white woman... You can do what you like to me because I have given myself to you. I don't have nowhere to go. So you taking advantage... [...] "is white skin you want" (p. 127)) she is not able to point to the contradictions between his radical anti-colonial posturing and his deeply colonised mentality. Veering between passive-aggressive laments about the humiliations of her powerlessness and childish threats ("I'll pester your life as you pester mine, make you unhappy as you make me unhappy"), Phyllis cannot phrase her complaints in a way that makes connection with him. When we see her through Peter's eyes ("crying, no longer fighting, no longer quarrelling, no longer threatening, reproaching, imploring, had just stood there crying, like the little girl he once had known" (p. 46)), St Omer points both to the powerlessness she feels, and the, at best, paternalistic way Peter sees her. The terms in which she accuses him ("You behave like this an you call Christ's name. You're a devil, that's what you are, a devil" (p. 47)), speak from the magical-religious world Peter feels he has long left behind, and serves only to accentuate the impossibility of their connection. She has not recognised that the Peter she married is, through his education and time away, no longer the same person. This is made clear when Jeannine compares him to her former lover, Marcel. She reflects on her understanding of Marcel's restlessness after his long time away in France. As she tells Peter, "There was no place on the island that had been his, to which he belonged and was a part of, and which, leaving France, he could return to. And, on his island, he had returned only to that which he had become in France" (p. 41). Peter has also come back to the region what he has become in London, a man who no longer connects or belongs. (It is a theme explored more explicitly in Lamming's character, Mark Kennedy in *Of Age and Innocence* and Orlando Patterson's Alexander Blackman in *An Absence of Ruins*.)[7] On the one hand, England has made Peter other, but, on the other, back in the West Indies what he has learnt in England seems meaningless. This division in Peter's psyche is suggested by the gap between his non-verbal feelings and his intellectual response to Phyllis's pain. When he finds himself weeping freely, he is left "wondering that he cried". The hyperbole of the thought that comes into his head when Phyllis accuses him of being a devil, ("He looked out at the dark. It seemed he had been hearing her voice for centuries" (p. 47) reverberates with feelings he cannot articulate. St Omer does not make this explicit, but the thought connects with Peter's childhood terror and fascination with the devil masquerade figure (qv. *Nor Any Country*), perhaps to the terrors taught by the church of his childhood.

St Omer's narrative of how Peter's and Phyllis's marriage breaks down repays attentive reading for its sensitivity to the undercurrents and silences in the relationship, and for the way that the scrupulous restraint of the prose creates passages that are deeply moving in their sympathies for both parties.

The second part of the Peter/Phyllis narrative begins with the very words that end *Nor Any Country* (before the couple's departure from St Lucia) on a note of ambivalence between Phyllis's optimism, expressed in the declaration that she might be pregnant, and Peter's suppression of the poisoned feelings that this news arouses, carrying him back to his suspicion that Phyllis trapped him into marriage by allowing herself to be made pregnant and then refusing to have an abortion (though the twins she carries die soon after their birth). There isn't in fact a pregnancy at this point of their departure for Jamaica, but the issue of contraception becomes a constant battle between them that Peter concedes only when he no longer cares what happens. His reluctance to have a child connects both to the "mist of renewed suspicion" of entrapment and to his class and cultural contempt that rules Phyllis out as a suitable mother for his child (he thinks son). He sees:

> their child, his and Phyllis's, going daily with others to church, and building a dependence that would last for ever on states of guilt, on the idea of sin and punishment and self-destroying remorse; on secrecy and hypocrisy, hope and apathy, and the expectation of reward in another life for the hardships of this one. He could not conceive, after the child that he had been, that a child of his should be ignorant or unaware. And Phyllis, as mother of a child who was aware, he could not imagine. (p. 91)

Whilst his desire to make Phyllis happy is presented as genuine (a response, no doubt, to his guilt over how he ignored her suffering whilst in England), what we don't see from Peter is any examination of why he treated her in this way. Instead, he wants the impossible, for "his world and Phyllis's, to exist by itself, closed and apart from the one about them" (p. 84). But, of course, he cannot prevent the contamination between these worlds. He is also inclined to see their difficulties as arising from his discontent with teaching at the university, his doubting that it serves any useful purpose. At first, domesticity seems a refuge, "the only protection against the increasing questioning of his motives for holding on to his appointment" (p. 84). This interpretation distracts him from the lie he is living, that he can, or wants to, bridge the actual divide between them. It is this failure, I think, that St Omer wants us to see as the fundamental reason for his despairing discontent. And whilst he keeps the narrative focused on the sad comedy of the books that Peter buys for Phyllis, which she pretends to read, but falls asleep over, and his flattering illusions that he is bringing her enlightenment ("for a brief moment, the lighted room (and themselves within it) was like a haven against the questioning of the worth of what he did and against the feeling of irrelevance and chaos which overwhelmed him every time he stepped out of the house" (p. 85)), the domestic space becomes the ground where an age-old Caribbean war is fought out. Despite Peter's self-perception as a man who rejects the "serpent's head of privilege others had created before them" (p. 88), even as he begins gilding and falsifying his memories of Anna, his first lover in London, he does not remember that Anna had once chided him "for wanting to pretend that he was what he was no longer and, after the education he had received, would never again become" (p. 89).

What is trapped in their university cottage is the whole post-emancipation history of the Caribbean and the massive divide between the socially privileged, largely pale minority (that belatedly admitted an even smaller minority of black West Indians to its ranks), educated in Euro-creole cultural values, and the largely black creole majority who cohered around greater or lesser fragments of African cultural residues. It is a divide that locates Peter in the world of colonial, western, rationalistic, abstract, logo-centric education, whilst as the narrative increasingly reveals, Phyllis remains part of what, seen from Peter's perspective, is a superstitious magico-religious world, whose thought processes are pre-abstract, whose modes are oral and deictic. To resurrect a term from the sociolinguistics of the period, whilst Peter speaks in what Basil Bernstein called an elaborated code,

Phyllis's codes are restricted[8] (though we later see that this is by no means true). In Peter's mind what he experiences with Phyllis reinforces his fears/prejudices of how little in the years since emancipation has the situation of the majority been developed:

> He discovered now that she was impatient with ideas and unwilling, or unable, to deal with them. She was comfortable only when she talked of things she had seen or heard or events that had happened to her or that she anticipated. She left her sentences unfinished, used exclamation and gesture more than the word. Her language was the language of a child, *or of a slave* to whom language had not been taught. When she spoke patois, she used English words; and the English she used was little more than transliterations of words and phrases from patois. *More than a century after Emancipation her language was still a makeshift one used not so much to express as to indicate"* [my italics] (p. 85).

Distressed by her lack of interest in the politics of anti-colonialism and black insurgency against the white world, Peter is further offended when she mentions that "she had seen strange black men loitering about. She believed, she said, they should get a dog" (p. 90). He begins to "regard himself as incomplete and ill-equipped with her as his wife", though his vision of an alternative is never other than "vague notions of relevant and meaningful action, something totally removed from what he was doing now, in a future that was as vague as the action he would pursue in it" (p. 91).

We can read in their relationship the divide between rulers and ruled, between the political classes who either slipped readily and cynically into the shoes of the departed colonial masters or who were idealistically frustrated by the people's stubborn reluctance to engage with modernity, and the masses whose engagement with nation-building sometimes went little further than voting for those who offered to lead them in the most charismatic ways. It is, of course, also the divide between the Caribbean novelist and those whose world they have attempted to interpret and sometimes ventriloquize. It is in this respect that it is obviously pertinent to look at how St Omer writes about Phyllis and her increasingly active role in the novel.

Here, we may note that by locating Phyllis within the Peter-focused third person narrative, St Omer closes down some of his options. Whilst she has the agency of action, apart from what she says (which Peter mostly refuses to listen to), we have no access to her thoughts, and see her almost wholly through Peter's eyes. For instance, there is a scene (pp. 111-114) where Phyllis is trying to tell Peter her dream, which he blanks out, so that we never know what it is, only that it "was finished". One might wish for more at this point, though I think it is worth remembering that in at least one of St Omer's previous novels (Anne Marie in *A Room on the Hill*) he shows a capacity for exploring an admirably intelligent woman character's thoughts in a rewarding way. Perhaps, we have to accept (though regret) that St Omer is more concerned to show that Phyllis is *not* given the domestic space for inward thought than to explore what those thoughts might be. I think that if St Omer can be accused of limitations in his portrayal of Phyllis, they have less to do with gender than with education and class. It is worth comparing this aspect of the novel with what Orlando Patterson achieves in exploring the inwardness of Dinah, in *The Children of Sisyphus* (1964) where, though she is even less educated and from an lower social strata than Phyllis, the reader has greater access to her inner thoughts.

There are three stages in the way St Omer characterises Phyllis from the point where she starts confronting Peter's withdrawal and his relationship with Jeannine. We see her first within a Fanonian context of acts of frustrated violence, of bouts of derangement ("She fell to the floor, rigid, her eyes closed, her arms stretched out along her sides, speechless, frothing at the mouth" (p. 95)). We are in the presence here of Fanon's "maleficent spirits which intervene every time a step is taken in a wrong direction".[9] There is the scene when Phyllis has tricked Peter into thinking that she is going to abort: "A witch had cast a spell on her. That was why she lost all her children. And that was why, she looked and smiled at him, she had married him, a devil." Then she runs around madly in the moonlight, ducking from his grasp:

> "You thought it was true," she said, breathing heavily, "you wanted it to be true. I fooled you. I fooled you. How I fooled you!"
> She was like a fairy gone mischievously mad in the moonlight.

[…]She was a child who had successfully played a trick on its favourite adult.
"I fooled you. I fooled you." (p. 98)

But there is another Phyllis who emerges in the lulls in their fighting when she tells him about her family past, a little of which he listens to, much of which he ignores. This is Phyllis speaking, and not as seen through Peter's perceptions. The stories she tells reveal a woman who is far more perceptive than we have so far been allowed to see. She has insights into the ways her home worked, its spatial divisions, her mother and father's roles, their position with respect to their neighbours. It reminds us (it isn't pointed out but is there to see) that hers is a story of thwarted opportunity, her schooling ended through her family's dire poverty after her father's death and then her pregnancy.

The penultimate images of Phyllis are of a woman driven beyond passive suffering to fight back against Peter and more particularly Jeannine, whom she beats so severely she has to be taken to hospital. St Omer presents these episodes in a neutrally factual way. We don't know what Phyllis is thinking. She just acts. But it is worth noting how this section of the novel has been read by at least a couple of its women readers. In the context of praising St Omer for his seriousness in dealing with the West Indian male sensibility, Velma Pollard and Pam Mordecai, in a joint interview, comment on this episode with considerable delight, on how Phyllis, in Pam Mordecai's words, "Absolutely decimate the white lady", how it is "the nicest thing in that book".[10] (There is also some discussion in the interview of the "syndrome" of the black male's attraction to white women.)

This episode, though, is not the last in the novel, which shows Phyllis as mother, suckling her child, watching as Peter sits in a chair drinking, watching him as he sits on the toilet, watching as he stares into the mirror. This is after his return home from the hospital to see Jeannine. It is a characteristically St Omerian ending, rich in ambivalence. Is Peter's gaze the belated beginnings of honest self-examination, or simply a further indication of his narcissism? Is the image of Phyllis and their child one of her endurance and their possibility (since Peter can't deny the pleasure he takes in the child), or one that signifies the unbridgeable divisions between them? What we may conclude, with more certainty, is that Phyllis has entered the narrative on her own terms and in pursuit of her own interests as she sees them. She has nowhere else to go. She watches and watches. She has no more illusions about Peter. But will she call Peter to account for his lies and self-deceptions?

There are, of course, two endings to the novel. The first is the final paragraph of the letter that Paul writes, signing off from his encounter with the masqueraders and his reflections on what he has witnessed. It is an uncomfortable conclusion, but one that involves both conscious choice (in existential terms) and truth. Its final tag, if Peter were ever to see it, would be a reminder that he, too, is his father's son, and that honest self-examination has to begin with that recognition:

> They say I'm mad. I know it's only that I have chosen a way to live with my confusion, and with the pain that results from my inability to solve it.
> Just like your father. (p. 125)

Characteristically, in the final scene in the novel, Peter's critical faculties are turned outward rather than inward, to reflect on the mediocrity of the local performance of an opera he has recently seen with Jeannine. It "reminded him of a picture he had once seen, of slaves celebrating their independence, dressed in the clothes of those who had enslaved them and who soberly watched them celebrate (p. 131). St Omer leaves us wondering from whose point of view Peter looks: the celebrating ex-slaves or the sober masters who are still very much in charge. We are left wondering whether he can summon the honesty to truly look within.

Notes

1. *The Complete Poems of Paul Laurence Dunbar* (New York: Dodd, Mead & Company, 1913), p. 71.
2. See *Black Skin, White Masks* (London: MacGibbon & Kee, 1967), pp. 147-150, 191-194.
3. *Jamaica Journal* 4 (June 1970), pp 34-48.
4. In St Omer's later novel, *Prisnms*, written in the USA in the 1980s-1990s and published in 2015 by Peepal Tree, one of the tropes is

how middle-class brown St Lucian, C.B., becomes Red, the outlaw denizen of a black ghetto in the USA, whereas Red Bam (the illegitimate son of an Indian prostitute and a white sailor) who passes for white, becomes the respectable business man, Frederick Olsen.

5. This feature of carnival performance (in this instance of a beast held in ropes by restraining dragons) is one that the Trinidadian author Ismith Khan uses in similarly suggestive ways in his novel, *The Obeah Man* (London: Hutchinson, 1964), see pp. 124-125.

6. It is interesting, though I make no supposition of any element of writing *á clef*, to encounter a comment by Roderick Walcott in an interview about his activities in St Lucia where he, like Peter, led a steelband, and had a boundary-crossing involvement with popular culture. He characterises himself as having "an African concept of life", whereas his brother Derek and Garth St Omer (then a good friend of Derek Walcott) "have a kind of European concept". See Olivier Stephenson, *Visions and Voices: Conversations with Fourteen Caribbean Playwrights* (Leeds: Peepal Tree Press, 2013), p. 371.

7. In *An Absence of Ruins* (Leeds: Peepal Tree Press, 2012), first published 1967, there is an intensive focus on how its anti-hero, Alexander Blackman, is wholly decentred by his long experience of England.

8. See Basil Bernstein, *Class, Codes and Control: Theoretical Studies Towards a Sociology of Language* (London: Routledge & Kegan Paul, 1971).

9. Frantz Fanon, *The Wretched of the Earth* (London: Penguin Ed., 1965), p. 43.

10. Daryl Cumber Dance, *New World Adams: Conversations with West Indian Writers* (Leeds: Peepal Tree, 1984, 2008), pp, 193-194. (The interviewees get Phyllis's name wrong in the interview).

PAUL TO PETER

I have been writing this in what used to be your wife's
room and had been yours before you left. That is where
the desk was and I did not bother to remove it. That desk!
I had had it made soon after I left school and began to
teach because it was on it that I was going to do the work
that would contribute to my future excellence. I hardly
used it. After my affair you took it over and when you
went away it remained in the room with Phyllis. After a
while your picture in cap and gown stood upon it. I used
sometimes to see it through the half-open door.

The desk is as new as I remember it. The grain of the
expensive wood shows clearly beneath the varnish. There
is no mark of ink, no scratch on its surface. As if you, and
Phyllis, and Time, had conspired to preserve it for me as
memory. I write on it at night after your father is asleep.

I am less and less sure that it is for you that I write. I
look forward to the moments when I am alone in this
room made hot because of the too-bright bulb and the
windows closed against insects. But I dread the times
when everything seems to rush out of my memory. I am
unable to cope with the outpouring. I put out the light,
open the windows, and go outside for a walk, donning
the pose of my madness to do so.

At other times, when what I write is less memory than
examination and evaluation, there is an orderliness and

a sequential lack of haste that suits me. I sit then and write for hours, forgetting myself, pleased with the feeling of control over what I write about events which once overwhelmed me. The orderly pace of my reflections and of my thoughts reassure me.

Yet, there is enough in what I have written to overwhelm me when I reread it, enough to make it likely I shall never send this to you, enough to make it imperative that, for my own sake, I send it to you, since I cannot send it to anyone else – as indictment, perhaps, but, more, as explanation.

Take, for instance, this episode which this moment comes to me and which I had long forgotten. I doubt your mother ever forgot it. But she is dead now and I shall never know. It happened at about the same time that I had bought the expensive and fine-grained wood to have the desk and the bookshelf made. It was, I remember, a Wednesday, St Mary's College Sports Day, the first Sports Day since I had left school. You had had only a moderate success because you had not trained and I remember being secretly pleased that you would not be proclaimed, as I had been the year before, Victor Ludorum.

About the middle of the meeting someone asked me to take part in the Old Boys' race. It was to be a 4 x 110 yards relay. I accepted to run. But, as the time for the race approached, I became more and more tense. In the other team were two Old Boys who had been school champions before me. I had not trained and, even though I had been school champion only a year before, was afraid to run. The other seven runners were drinking and exchanging jokes before the bar at the back of the pavilion. I could hear them from where I sat with two boys who had left school together with me. The young men I listened to were not my friends. I had shared neither in their drinking nor in their jokes. It was obvious that they had asked me to run because of my speed and that the race, for them, was mere fun. But I did not want to lose. I spent all the time before the race began trying to assess the two teams and when the race was about to begin I was terrified.

It did not help that I had to run the last leg. The race began. At the second changeover the other team, which had been leading slightly, dropped the baton. Our team moved ahead. I received the baton, put my head down, and ran as for my life. I felt as if I had won that race singlehandedly. We went afterwards to the home of one of the runners to share the cake that was the prize. Other Old Boys and some ex-Convent girls joined us. There was liquor and beer and soft drinks. I was speaking to many of the people in that room for the first time. I felt I had begun to arrive, begun to be an Old Boy in the real sense of the word.

When I went home your mother was just coming out of the kitchen. She had cleared the table where you had eaten and was preparing it for me. She was singing "Sweet Heart of Jesus, Fount of Love and Mercy". I said, "Good night, Ma," and went upstairs to bathe and dress. I was going to the cinema for I had been unable to see the film on Sunday and I did not want to miss it again. I do not remember the name of the film. It is lost along with the other names of the scores of American films that I felt it my duty at that period to go to see. When I came downstairs again, my jacket on my arm, my tie thrown loosely over the collar of my shirt, the table was laid for me. I sat down before it. Our mother, singing her hymn, was sitting in her favourite chair, a booklet of prayers in her hand. You had, as usual, told her nothing about what had taken place on the sports field. I wanted to tell her about the race and, especially, about how I had felt at the party afterwards. She seemed remote. I felt I could tell her nothing she could understand or was interested in. She was still singing. But it was clear that she was not interested in, and paid no attention to, the words she uttered. That she was thinking about something else while she sang.

I uncovered a dish. Fried fish with rings of half-fried onions and tomatoes lay on a plate. Under a cloth the bread was already sliced. Drops of perspiration had formed on my forehead. In front of me the jug of cocoa steamed. Unless I got out into the open soon I should be wet. Suddenly, it was like coming back home after playing cricket on another island. I felt I did not deserve this. I was contributing now to the cost of running the house. I said so, pushing back my chair and getting up from the table. I opened a window wide before I began to put on my tie. But the slight breeze on my face was not enough to cool me. I said I was tired of fried fish and bread morning noon and night. Your mother, who had stopped her singing, did not correct my exaggeration. I said I was tired of soup, made from bones, every Sunday night. Your mother, the booklet in her hands, watched me silently from her chair, not seeing as I did, the meals I had had in hotels on other islands where I had stayed with the rest of the team. Exaggerating the cause of my dissatisfaction, I did not notice her reproach. I finished putting on my jacket and went outside…

What is there more to say? I have written this exactly as it has come back to me. Had it been longer, I should have stopped writing and gone outside to walk in the night. I cannot be sure that the perspiration on my face comes only from the bulb next to me and the heat of the closed room.

It is memories like this one that overwhelm me, memories that, unsolicited, come to interrupt the orderly letter that I had planned to write.

PETER & PHYLLIS

"I heard from Marcel today," Jeannine said.

"Your fiancé?"

"Ex-fiancé, you mean. No. That was Jacques. Marcel's the other one. He wants me to come over for the holidays… I should go… don't you think?"

Peter said nothing.

"Well?"

"That's you decision."

"Don't be like that, Peter."

"Isn't it?"

"Of course it is, but…"

She did not finish. Instead she said:

"Maybe I should go. That will give things here a chance to settle. I may even forget Phyllis's slaps."

But Peter remained silent and she added: "I'm sorry, Peter. I didn't have to say that."

And:

"Marcel will give me his red sports car. I'll live in his new house out of the town. On mornings I'll go down to his private beach…"

She stopped speaking. The music from the sitting-room floated through the curtained doorway on the silence between them. The sound of flute and clarinet was like the playful scurry of lizards on a sunlit veranda. And Peter, recognizing the concerto and humming, remembered a room in London and tea and cake with Anna. Ultimately, she would have to come back, to leave the museums and the art-galleries and the concert-halls of Europe and, fleeing the alienation and frustrations of metropolitan society, rediscover the alienation and the frustrations of her own.

Jeannine, still quiet, lay on the bed next to him. She knew intimately the signs of his withdrawal, the humming, and the fingers moving restlessly – on the mattress now, on a table in a restaurant, a bar they sat on high stools before at three or four in the morning, or, soundlessly, on the steering-wheel, against the noise of the engine of his car climbing the quickly rising foothills in a late afternoon. Even against the stories related on campus by staff and students alike, of his extreme brutality towards Phyllis, he looked vulnerable. But she had learned the folly of being sympathetic and, as if to control her affection for him, she tried to imagine the cruelty she had heard people speak of but had herself not known.

"I'd much prefer to stay here with you," she said.

He looked at her. But she turned away from the contradictions of his open face – from the nose that was flat, the forehead too broad and bulging, the eyes that were both dead and piercing. She preferred the single, uncomplicated line of his face in profile.

In the beginning of their relationship he had been preoccupied with happiness and responsibility. Continuously, more than ever when he was very drunk, he had urged her to be happy. Man would never be happy, he repeated, until he became responsible, not to a god or an idea, but to himself and to his fellowman. Responsibility was what education must be about. Over drinks before bars, driving to the beach or up into the hills, lying next to her after they had made love, he had talked and talked – about man's inhumanity to man, about racism, exploitation, and greed. He had talked about the islands, called them anachronisms; made fun of the towns, ex-depots, become, suddenly, as if transformed by the wand of a fairy, cities, no different from the towns they replaced, the keys to which colourfully robed mayors presented at spectacular ceremonies. He had spoken of the Shadow Politics and the Shadow Religions – all unexamined, none understood, that separated and divided, and sapped strength that might have been collective. And he had sneered at independence as it seemed the leaders of the islands understood it. Independence, he maintained, no more than Emancipation, had been achievement. The slaves had not acquired one nor the island governments the other. But they had made of another's expedient conces-sion their own achievement and were proud of it.

"We are like children," he used to say, "mindlessly imitating adults, informing our fantasy with total and high seriousness. We not only make cakes out of mud. We eat them as well. We are so busy imitating others that we have no time to do anything of our own."

Then suddenly he had become silent. Increasingly he had come to her, after the drinking elsewhere, to make love and, afterwards, lie silently next to her and drink some more. If he came early enough to her, he fell asleep and awakened her later to make love again before going. When they went to the hills now, they left the car and walked along paths up which she was unable to follow him. And on the beach, discarding her near the shore, he swam far out, returning, much later, to dive again and again, and swim for long minutes underwater.

It was as if the problems he had talked despairingly about to her had disappeared and all that remained was this physical activity that seemed never to tire him. And, increasingly, it had been she who spoke to him. She got down from the bed.

"Another beer, Peter?"

He nodded and she went through the curtained doorway. When she appeared again in the bedroom, he sat up, his back against the wooden partition, and took the bottle she handed him.

"Marcel's like you," she said. "He never looks as if he belongs, no matter where he is."

She sat on the floor, her back against the bed and to him.

"He told me once that France had been just a room full of people at a party. His scholarship was enabling him to pass through it with his overcoat and his gloves on… He has property now on the island, and a view."

She remembered it. It was magnificent. Marcel had driven her out to see it early on the morning of her departure. After about twenty minutes the red sports car had left the tarred road and bumped over a path which a man and his two teen-aged sons were widening and clearing with cutlasses. She and Marcel had had to leave the car and walk over the tractor tracks for the final two or three hundred yards. They had stood in the noise of the tractor and he had pointed to where the tree-covered land seemed to give place suddenly to the sea distantly below them.

"There's a beach below there, my private beach. But there's no road yet. You'll see it when you come back. It's beautiful. And you'll have it all to yourself."

He waved to the driver of the tractor which lumbered noisily. The man waved back smiling broadly.

"This is where I'm going to build," Marcel said, "where we're standing… And if I build high enough I could cut off their view."

He pointed; and for the first time she had noticed that there were two large houses behind and to the left of where they were standing.

"But I have no choice. It's the only way that I can get the most of my own view and be able to see my beach from a window."

She agreed. She was impressed. The tractor rumbled, clearing the ground it moved over. She watched the black man manipulate it.

"They tried to double-cross me on the property," Marcel said. "They found out I was interested and offered the owner, the man we just passed working with his sons, twice the amount I had thought of offering him."

Then he had laughed.

"I thought quickly. I had taken an option on the property. I told him it was an agreement to sell to me and that if he sold to anyone else I could take him to court. I frightened him, poor fellow. I am a lawyer. And he cannot read. I settled the deal quickly. I borrowed money, mortgaged my house in town. I made my parents – a pity you didn't have time to see them, you'll see them next time – I made them mortgage the small piece of land they have in the country. And I began to clear the place at once. The next time you come it will be ready for you."

They watched the tractor uproot a particularly big tree stump. Its snapped roots were yellowed and many. "You know who owns those houses?" Marcel asked. And, without waiting for an answer, he told her: "Jacques owns one. A retired civil servant, a Frenchman, owns the other."

He had smiled.

"Marcel raped me once," Jeannine told Peter now.

But he said nothing and, sipping her beer, she told him about it. It was summer. Jacques had graduated and returned to the island. She would follow a year later, when she and Marcel would finish, to marry him. She went to see Marcel in his room one day and he held her with his long, strong arms…

"I couldn't understand it," she said to Peter, "he and Jacques were friends. Besides, he knew that we were engaged."

She had written Jacques who never answered her and, three years later, when she had the opportunity to come down to the islands, she had taken it. She had travelled by the French Line because she knew that Jacques's island was the first one the ship would touch at.

"I wanted so much to see Jacques again," she said.

That night Jacques's sister, Therese, had met her at the door, let her in, then excused herself to fetch her mother. Jeannine had sat alone in a large, illuminated sitting-room and looked, above shelves filled with books, from picture to picture, upon a succession of mulatto faces, of men and women, who seemed to be examining her. Overwrought, expecting to see Jacques enter the room at any moment, she had waited for what seemed an age before the voluminous and stately woman had appeared. And while she waited in the glare of electric candles from the overhanging chandelier each painted face she looked at had made her feel more and more uncomfortable. There was not a single black face, she went on, nor a white one. As if they had always been mulattos and the strain had always existed, separately and by itself.

Jacques's mother told her that he had been back in France for over a year. Jeannine had felt hurt and a fool. For the first time she understood how little Jacques had intended to marry her. And how much, all along, Marcel had known it.

"That room," she said, "with the portraits on the walls smelled of tradition and allegiance. Everything – the furniture, the clothbound books, the old-fashioned French courtesy of the little girl, Therese – everything spoke of preservation and continuity. It was all important, too important ever to be discarded easily. I had a strong feeling of seventeenth-century France, of determination, even of reprisal."

"Reprisal?" His question surprised her. In a way she had been talking to herself.

"Yes. Jacques's wife will have to be mulatto. Or else… I could feel that 'or else'. In his mother's extreme but formidable politeness, in the portraits that intimidated me…"

And then, slowly:

"I had never considered exclusion. I was shocked. I had assumed I should be welcome. I had fought my father over Jacques. He was an Italian who had come to France and had married my mother, a maid. In time they had owned the small café in the little town where we lived. I hated that town and I did not know Italy. I was looking for tradition. And allegiance. Jacques spoke of coming back to take his father's place. Listening to him, I recognized a place that had been taken by a succession of sons before him. I was eager to come down and take my place by his side and give him the son that would succeed him…"

She sipped her beer.

"I left that room hurt and confused. I felt again the little girl I used to be who wore braces on her teeth and looked at herself all the time in the mirror. I should have gone back for it was to see Jacques that I had come. But I had signed a contract. I was going to be here for two years. After a week, I wrote Marcel telling him where I was and how I had spent a few hours on his and Jacques's island. He invited me to come back and spend Christmas on it with him. I went."

Marcel, blacker and without his beard, was waiting for her at the airport. He enfolded her with his long, strong arms and laughed. He said:

"Have you forgiven me?"

It seemed, Jeannine told Peter, he was referring to a mild and long forgotten prank.

Marcel lived in a house, in the centre of the town, that was much too large for him. His parents lived in the country. He promised and promised, but there had never been time, during her two weeks on the island, for him to take her to visit them. He abandoned his house to her, came with his red sports car to collect her every day. They went around the island, to the mountains in its centre, to the beaches. Every, night they had made love. He had been as restless as a wild stallion let loose again in a strange field. In time she had understood his restlessness. There was no place on the island that had been his, to which he belonged and was a part of, and which, leaving France, he could return to. And, on his island, he had returned only to that which he had become in France.

"But perhaps," she said now to Peter, "his children will inherit that house with the view of the private beach and begin a tradition and allegiance all of their own."

And Peter:

"And in the meantime what about the man and his two sons cutting his path for him?"

Jeannine did not answer. In France Jacques had talked to Marcel and herself about the year he had spent managing the family estate. On a Saturday, driving in the jeep, he would be hailed by a group of workers who wanted him to give them a ride. He would "deposit them at the nearest rumshop and fill them up with white rum. We really used to get along. They knew I was their friend. We used to eat together."

She got up from the floor.

"There's no more beer, Peter. I think I shall go and get some."

"I'll come with you."

"No. I'll be right back. Want anything? Cigarettes?"

"No."

She had picked up her dress from the floor and was slipping it over her head and shoulders when they heard the knock on the front door. They looked at each other, then Jeannine went out towards the renewed knocking. Peter heard Phyllis ask:

"Is Dr. Breville here?"

"No, he isn't."

He could hardly hear Jeannine's voice above the music but Phyllis's was firm and raised as if she directed it at him sitting on Jeannine's bed.

"I haven't seen my husband since morning."

"He isn't here."

"He's not in his office. His car's in the garage."

"Mrs. Breville, I know nothing of your husband."

"Good night."

He heard the sound of Phyllis's footsteps move away. Jeannine came into the bedroom and sat on the edge of the bed.

"Did you lock the door?"

She shook her head.

"Go and lock it."

"Shouldn't you go home?" she asked when she returned.

"Not now. Why don't you get the beer?"

"All right."

"And lock the door."

She went out of the bedroom. He heard the noise of the key in the lock and, a little later, of the small car leaving the garage. The music had stopped but the turntable, turning still, made a slight noise. Phyllis's voice rose above it.

"Peter, let's go home. I know you there. Let's go."

Her voice was pitched low, as confident and persuasive as a priest's, and he distrusted it. He drank the last of his beer.

"I'm waiting for you."

He listened.

"I'm waiting. But I can't keep the child in the dew like that. She'll get sick. Let's go home."

He sat, his back against the wooden partition, his legs pulled up in front of him, his hands, one holding the empty bottle, around his knees.

"I know you inside. Come out."

Her voice was still low. The door shook. He heard the knob turn, then turn again. He did not move.

"She lock the door, but you can open it if you want."

Silence for a while.

"You not coming out?"

The door shook again.

"I don't want to make a noise, Peter."

Quiet. And then the rattling of the door louder than ever.

"Come out, come out."

He recognized the sound of the small car returning. The slap of Phyllis's footsteps moved away from the apartment door. He was relieved to hear Jeannine lock the door behind her. She came into the bedroom.

"You didn't change the record…" she began.

He told her about Phyllis.

"She knows you're here."

"Of course, she knows."

"I'm going now." Phyllis's voice came loudly from behind the locked door. "But you'll see, both of you."

They heard the sound of her slippers diminish as she moved away.

"I'd like a beer," Peter said.

"Walking with the child…" Jeannine began.

But Peter did not want to talk about it and told her so. They drank beer in silence and listened to the music she had put on again. It was perhaps an hour afterwards that he said:

"It's almost two. I'd better go."

He was on his feet. After he had dressed, he put a hand on Jeannine's head and passed his fingers through the thin strands that were so different from the thick heaviness of Phyllis's mulatto hair. He felt Jeannine shudder as his hand lingered over the prickly stubs of cut hair high on her neck. He raised her from where she was sitting on the floor, her back against the bed, and lifted the dress over her up-stretched arms. Then he took her on the edge of the bed, his clothes on.

"I must go."

She was lying on the bed now.

"Turn off the player."

"And the light?"

"Leave it on."

She was smoking a cigarette.

He went out of the apartment and down the concrete steps to the ground. A few yards from the building, he heard the familiar, uneven fall of Phyllis's footsteps begin behind him.

She followed him without speaking all the way to the

house. The door was locked. But there was something accusatory, justified, even magnanimous, in the gesture she would make to open it and he did not want to see it. He stood for a while on the veranda and turned to the door only when he had heard the noise of the key in the lock. He entered and sat down in the sitting-room before going to his bedroom. But he did not bother to put the chair behind the door. He wanted the violence he expected to take place quickly. He lay on the bed, fully clothed, and waited for the door to burst open, for the light to come on. After a while, he heard Phyllis unlocking the door of his room. The key grated in the lock. He was amazed that she should have found the key where he had hidden it. He sprang up to meet her, fully awake again, to discover that he had dozed and to remember that, when Phyllis came, there would be no grate of key in lock since, long ago, she had taken all the keys in the house and hidden them. It was the click of the switch, rather than the light from which he turned to face the wall, that awakened him the second time. Her voice was low, of one tone. Only its pace was hurried.

"You leave me here with the child alone and go to your women... you leave me like a dog, and go to your white woman... You can do what you like to me because I have given myself to you. I don't have nowhere to go. So you taking advantage..."

He felt the sheet move beneath him as she pulled on it.

"You think you can spend the night with your woman and come here and go to sleep just like that?"

He turned from the wall and looked squintingly at her. Her breasts moved up and down. Her long hair fell partly in front of, and partly behind her shoulder. If he held her, said he was sorry, she would let him sleep, would lie down herself to sleep beside him.

"Because I don't have nowhere to go, you doing this…"

In one of their early fights she had thrown herself again and again at him, had been hurled away to rebound off the edge of the dining-table, or fall over one of the coffee-tables near the armchairs, had rushed again and again into his thrusting hands, springing up from where she had suddenly found herself sitting on the floor to run towards his retreating back and half-turn him with a hand on his shoulder, had been brushed aside and sent reeling among the jumbled furniture, without a word or any show of anger by him, and, in the end, had stood crying, no longer fighting, no longer quarrelling, no longer threatening, reproaching, imploring, had just stood there crying, like the little girl he once had known.

Squinting he looked at her as at another piece of furniture then turned again to face the wall. And he was lying, his back to her and to her words, when he felt the mattress almost pulled from beneath him. He got up from the bed, not looking at her, took his cigarettes, and went on to the veranda. He smoked, leaning over the wooden railing and looking at the dark. And as he stood in the cool listening to her talk about how she had given herself to him and how, since she had no place for her to go to, he could do with her what he wanted, treat her like a dog, as if she was not a human being, he felt the tears, quite suddenly, flow down his face. He smoked, listening to her, hunched over the railing, wondering that he had cried, aware that he could not face her. He composed his voice and said:

"Phyllis, for Christ's sake…"

"For Christ's sake yourself. What you know of Christ? You behave like this and you call Christ's name. You're a devil, that's what you are, a devil."

He looked out at the dark. It seemed he had been hearing her voice behind him for centuries.

"Don't trouble trouble and trouble won't trouble you. You treat me like a dog. You don't speak to me. You come and go as if I'm not in the house. As if I'm a piece of wood. I've given myself to you. You know I have nowhere to go. You take advantage. You trouble me all the time. You're nothing but a devil. A wicked devil."

He felt very tired. Violence had achieved nothing. He could only appeal to Phyllis now. It was impossible to pretend she did not exist. It would be so easy if she, too, had wished to pretend that he did not exist.

"Phyllis," he said, "what's the use?"

He was surprised to hear the unaccustomed sound of her laughter behind him.

"Go home," he said, meaning their island, "go back home, Phyllis. Take Michael and the baby with you. Go and see your mother…"

She stopped laughing and did not let him finish.

"That's what you want. I'll never leave here. Never. Not even if I had a place to go to. But you know I don't have. So you laughing. You telling me to go to my mother…"

He sat down in the veranda chair. The hole in the armrest suggested a drink. He remembered, almost out of the chair, that he kept no drink now in the house and had not bothered to find out where she kept hers. She came and stood in front of him.

"Listen to me. I not going nowhere. Not even if you kill me. I not going. I not going."

Her voice which had begun low ended in a scream. The dark of the night was giving way to intimations of the day about to begin. Somewhere, a too-early cock crowed. It was not answered.

"You have a child, you don't care. You don't come home to eat. You leave the house in the morning and you come back four the next one. And you say you educated. You're doctor. Is so doctors does behave? You see anybody else doing that that have family? Every whore that come, you after them. And if they white, better yet. You not thinking about your family at all. And you telling me go home. Where you think my home is? Eh? I not going nowhere you hear ? Nowhere. I not going nowhere. Go home! That's all you can say. Because you know I don't have nowhere to go, I don't have no family to go to. And you telling me to go back home! My home is here."

Once he would have jeered at, and taunted her; sent her to her brothers, to her mother's house, the big house that was a shambles now. He would have poured upon her all the resentment he felt for their marriage and the contempt for himself; the scared young man who had agreed to it.

"I won't leave you alone," she said. "I'll pester your life as you pester mine, make you unhappy as you make me unhappy."

It was getting lighter. Peter could make out the trunks of trees, the shapes of houses. More cocks crowed. He heard them beat their wings. He got up and went to the toilet. He did not bolt the door. He knew it was only a matter of time before Phyllis followed him and he preferred not to hear the sounds of her fists on the closed door nor of her shouts coming through it.

PAUL

Perhaps, Peter, you were too young to remember the old white man who passed in his car before our house on his way to work. Every day, taking him to his office in the town and back to his house on the hill, the black car, driven by the black, uniformed chauffeur, went serenely, unhurriedly by. He was the only white man I ever saw on our street who was not a sailor or a priest.

When we played, I remember, if I was a sailor, I could imagine I wore a sailor's uniform and pretend that the nonsense I uttered was an English accent. If I blessed, as a priest, it was with a hand of no specific colour, not even my own. But it showed out of colourful, wide-sleeved garments I invented for myself; and the gibberish I intoned aloud as I swung the imaginary censer was the private conversation of a priest with his god that I was too young to reproduce faithfully. But the old man passing daily in his car did not provide me with the transfiguring grace of word and dress to distinguish me from the child I was. I had never heard him speak. And the ordinary white drill that he wore was neither strange nor attractive to me. His remoteness only distinguished him. On Sunday afternoons, when we played in the weedy open space next to the market that Doux-doux took us to, if I was the old man, and you the driver – and you always were the driver – my unsmiling face looked straight beyond you along the mast we sat astride and which moved up and down as you jumped on it. My stern, authoritative silence, I hoped, was exactly like that of the old white man I had so carefully observed.

Your father, too, had observed him. Sometimes, I remember your father sitting before the open window of our house, in full view of the women whose children he god-fathered and whipped – the market vendors, the domestic servants, the sellers in shops and rum-shops, the fishmongers – sitting so obviously on display, his pipe in his mouth (as sometimes that old man had his pipe in his), the library book, which I subsequently discovered he had great trouble reading, open before him, and, immediately, the image of the stern, effigy-like old man, passing briefly, unconcernedly, in his car over the dirty street before our house, comes to replace your father's image in my mind. But it was many years before I heard your father express openly his admiration for the man he, too, imitated.

The old man had died. His son now drove himself to work. The black car was no longer special: other cars had begun to appear on the island. I had won a scholarship and was at St Mary's College. You were still preparing to take the scholarship examination; but you disliked going to private lessons and your father beat you often for avoiding them. I had learned the difference between the breezy hills where the old man's house had been and the hot, choked town in which we lived. In the town, I now played, sometimes, behind high walls topped with broken glass, in the concrete yards of huge houses my new friends lived in. I knew that the old man's son drank a great deal. But I probably would not have remembered the accident which he and the expatriate wife of another white islander had in the hills if I had not heard my father say:

50

"That boy. He has no damn ambition…"

It was a Sunday morning. I was dressing to go to High Mass. I recognized the tone of your father's voice, the anger in it that preceded the blow. I stood up from lacing my shoe and turned fearfully around. But I was overreacting, because of the tone and anger I had recognized. The raised voice was coming from over the partition behind which your father was talking to your mother. It had continued,

"…He's worthless. Nothing like his father."

Your father was speaking patois. His outburst of angry disapproval against that "boy", the old man's son whom he would have removed his warder's cap to speak to, was as natural as if, on my way to church, he had discovered that my shoes were not shining or that my hair was uncombed. He had used the word "worthless" many times to frighten and discipline us; and he was to use it many times more, later, to describe the friends, his godchildren among them, who did not go to school, and with whom, despite the floggings, you insisted on swimming in the harbour. But it was the first and only time I ever heard him use the phrase "nothing like his father".

That phrase I like to think of as an explanation. The children whom he godfathered and whipped, men and women now, do not come to see him. Their mothers do – still unmarried, still sellers in the market, and the shops, and the rum-shops, still domestic servants. They tell him about his godchildren as though it were he who had fathered them. Listening to them, sometimes, I forget that the children they talk about are adults now with children of their own. When they have gone, I look at his coal-black, lean face, the grey short hair, the frail body, and I wonder about the place he was born in, the life he led before he came here to become a warder in the capital, the reasons why he never went back, nor took us ever to, that place in the country he had come from and had never talked to us about. I wish then that we could be friends. I watch him sitting helplessly in his chair and am afraid to show that I am sorry or that I wish to understand. And I tell myself, sometimes, that he must be mad. For he bears the paralysis and the threatened other stroke too patiently; and resignation, submission, or despair, I cannot entertain as possible for him. Once, remembering his favourite position, I pushed his chair towards the window. The vehemence of his refusal, which he could not express in words, frightened me. It was as if he wished his new impotence not to be seen by those whom, for so many years, he had been posturing to.

I no longer hate him. Neither for his excesses nor for his pretence. I understand why he had to create his own world. You, too, must remember the contrast between the world we lived in near the market and the streets you walked along on a Sunday morning after Mass. Of those long, empty, sunlit streets, without dustbins or public stand pipes, I remember the quiet, not as an absence of noise, but as an unnatural intensification of the most ordinary sound. The water flowing in gutters that emerged from unseen yards, closed off by gates, seemed to shout at me secrets that were as attractive as they remained mysterious. The smell of food was always richer than the smell of food at home. The stretch of houses and intervening closed gates was orderly and private. And the bright sunlight, after the gloom within the church, always was like joy. I seem to hear the sound of trees as I write this and yet it can only be the feel of the wind that I remember coming down the empty streets from the hills. In that wind the heat was like a touch. I quickly forgot the murmurings I could not understand of the priest at the altar, his genuflexions and turnings before it, the ceremonial of his arms, showing out of wide-sleeved, colourful garments, opening and closing...

What impetus for make-believe I derived from those children's Masses! Even though, in the bright sunlight outside, I forgot the ritual at once, it could not have been more real while I was inside the vaulty church. If, aping the Irish nuns who taught us, I beat my breast and repeated phrases about my unworthiness, no one yearned more achingly than I to become worthy. And when I returned from the altar rails, head bent and hands clasped before me, I knew I was already in that other world which I would more properly inherit after my life on this one. Of that future world I knew nothing – not its shape, nor its feel, nor its smell. But it filled me with ecstasy. And it was infinitely more real than the tiled floor of the church I walked upon.

So, too, in time, I came to inhabit the world that jarred me so sharply by its difference from ours every time I came out of the church. The quiet, uncluttered streets were not my streets. The firm, well-painted houses with raised verandas, I had never set foot in. But I possessed them no less. The smells of shops and rum-shops where we lived disgusted me. I had taken your father's aversion and made it my own and my intolerance became more extreme than his had ever been. Not for me, as it had been for him, the façade of pipe-smoking serenity before an open window on a street he cursed and longed to get away from. Unlike him, I should reach for no external symbol for a world existing in my mind alone. Mine was no longer make-believe. Its reality was less for others to see than for me to possess. I wished to give the impression that I was a superior being endowed naturally with genius and with talent. Your father, our father, had had to make his own rules, out of his confusion, and to hope they should become meaningful to him, and to the equally confused whom he sought to impress and whom he despised. But if he was a pioneer, that freed me from needing to be one. I, therefore, spurned the confused and the perplexed: their admiration could mean nothing to me. Your father, smoking his pipe, like the old man in his car, had needed an uninterrupted exposure, and his window had provided it. He had not needed subtlety nor excellence. For, when a discarded sailor's uniform, or a chauffeur's suit was achievement, like the smoking of a pipe, what was the norm of excellence? And if raw anger and pure violence existed without rancour, where was the need for subtlety? I wished to be subtle, rather than obvious, and to have solid achievement, rather than shoddy facade. You know how hard I worked. Your father wanted to impress; I, to overwhelm.

Well… That had been my intention. Sometimes, I remember our mother selling fruits and ground provisions on boxes on the pavement before our house because we needed money and your father felt it was degrading and not respectable for her to continue to be a market vendor. I think of Doux-doux, the servant girl he insisted we get, whom we could not afford, and had been unable to keep. I remember, when your father was in the house, our having to look enviously from the window at the children who played on the pavement because we were not allowed to play on the streets. I remember more; the beating for a drinking-glass I had broken, the shorts you soiled too quickly, the coin I had set out to make a purchase with and had lost. I almost know again, now, that early need for carefulness, and the shrivelling anxiety that controlled it. If your monthly cheque is late, I wonder what would happen if it did not come at all. And yet, and yet, it was to avoid this that I had been single-minded...

That was why, for instance, years later, I refused to play in the school's steelband. You who, even after you had won a scholarship, still swam sometimes with your old friends in the harbour, did not care. Your father did not approve of your playing in the band. But he had begun to leave us alone. He no longer forced you to wear your shirt inside your pants. And, on Sunday mornings, you and your college friends swam in that very harbour for swimming in which you had so often been beaten in the past. As if the harbour had changed! The truth is that college had given us a special immunity against his disapproval. The initiative was passing away from him to you and me. Increasingly, our loyalties, our obedience, were not to him but to something else, a new authority that existed outside of the house and which he, too, respected but apprehended only vaguely.

But if he was becoming unsure about values, I was sure of the values the steelband represented and would have no part of them. Wednesday nights I stood outside the Methodist school building and listened to members of the Arts Society sing European songs, play the piano, and recite English verse. Standing apart from the other onlookers, my hands in my pockets, I moved ostentatiously even farther away from any giggle or remark that I thought was too loud. I did not want those inside who turned towards where the interruption had come from to see me. For I recognized their look – your father's and mine – of disapproval and contempt. Yet I knew that the middle-aged civil servants, teachers and clerks, dressed in suits and evening gowns and performing under the hot electric lights inside, could not see us who stood in the dark of the yard to observe them. Every Wednesday I came to look at them. And yet I knew they were failures, despite their costumes and their performances under the bright lights of the Methodist school building. They were not professionals – not doctors nor lawyers – and they were not white. And I did not therefore wish to become what they were. At the same time, even though my ambition soared beyond what they represented, their failure, which I acknowledged, held out for me a means of success. I knew that, if I wished, I, too, could stand up one day under the hot lights and that those others who watched with me would not be able to do so.

I would look around me. Young men and women of my age, but already working, stood singly or in pairs. There were elementary school teachers, shop assistants, policemen out of uniform, carpenters, even fishermen... If there was another college boy, we stood together, apart from the others, by ourselves. I had been to elementary school with many of those who watched with me but I no longer spoke to them. In the church I, as college boy, sat apart from them. I performed to their admiration on the playing-fields, but their shouts did not stand out from the general acclamation. I stood with them behind official ropes, because I had no choice, to watch parades on Columbus Square, parades I should have liked to be able to witness from the verandas of houses overlooking the Square. And, daily, I walked the streets, and measured my potential distance above, and my growing superiority to them. I would not play in the steelband to be enclosed by them, or by their friends.

So you can begin to understand how I felt that Carnival Tuesday when your band and its followers passed. I had just come from reading the foreign periodicals in the library and was sitting on a bench on the Square. How, even now, the quiet of that part of the town fascinates me! Even now, years later, when I hear a cock crow in memory, it is of a cock, not in our yard where the fowls walked over the clothes your mother had spread out on the bleaching stones, nor even in the house where they left their droppings on the floor for you or me to clean, but, on a Sunday mid-morning after Mass, crowing so unexpectedly from behind a closed gate on that quiet street that its sound still startles me.

So you will understand my mood as you passed with your band that afternoon. The sun had set and sitting down on the bench was like putting down a load that I had been carrying all day. Perhaps the volume of sound, and the confusion of actual sound and echo I seem to remember, is coloured by my resentment. The crowd, which in my mind sweeps from pavement to pavement, could not have been as large. I remember there was some space between its edge and where I sat alone and watched. For, across that space, one or two school mates had come to tap me playfully on the head and return to skip behind you. You passed, with all your noise, and I had a feeling of satisfaction that I was sitting on the bench. For the verandas of the houses in front of me were filled now with people who had come to watch you. I was glad that they could see me sitting alone on the bench. The noise you made still echoed confusingly. I felt reassured and vindicated, as if my dissociation from you had become tangible for those on their verandas to hold. I wanted to stand out to those who watched from their verandas, to be pointed at by them, to be included among those who watched but did not participate. I was sure of their disapproval. I wished them to be aware of my own. I stood up.

My memory of myself getting up from that bench is one of an exaggeratedly slow and deliberate movement, like that of a beggar lingering to be noticed. Getting measuredly off the bench, I had intended to walk nonchalantly in the opposite direction – towards the church and away from you. But my covert looks had shown that those looking from their verandas were turned towards you and I feared they might not see me. I wanted to be seen. Without any break in my movement I began to walk in the direction that you and your followers had taken.

Though I could no longer see you I knew, from the sounds that you made, that the band had stopped. The people in the verandas, some of them, were still watching you and I wondered what they were looking at. There was nothing to see from that distance that could not have been more completely seen while you were passing beneath them. From the bench, I had been able to see only the noisy, scuffling crowd that enclosed you. You who made the music, shuffling under the weight of your pans, I had neither seen nor heard. But from the high point of their verandas, those, whose attention I craved, had been able to see you within the enclosure the frenzied mob had formed. I wondered what they were looking at. Then I could see you again and I understood. The band had stopped in front of the Social Club to which many of the onlookers belonged.

Out of the corner of my eye I could see that the white observers among them had now all left their verandas. Their curiosity had been only fleeting. They had no representatives among you – not among those who jigged, and not among you who played for the jiggers to jig to. Their sons and daughters, with or without approval, were not among the musicians nor among the revellers. Their Social Club, built anew, was out of town.

There was, therefore, nothing – of interest or concern – to make them continue now to look over their veranda rails. It was the others alone, before whose club you and the mob had stopped, who looked at you.

I know that if all the people who lived around Columbus Square were white, as they once had been, I should not so much have sought their attention nor thought so covetously of one day living in houses like the ones they lived in. But, already, on those far away Sunday mornings, I had also seen those others whose brown skins, indeterminate between black and white, had intimidated me no less than the white skins of their neighbours. The houses, the aproned maids, the shiny brass knobs – all had seemed interchangeable. Beyond the complexional variation I could not tell difference. To me, at that time, there was no difference.

I don't know whether you can remember the church organist, the frail, old white man with white hair and a white moustache. I remember him stepping delicately among us who, having come early in order to get a seat, sat on the wooden steps that led to the choir loft. It was a feast day. The church was packed. Your mother and I had come an hour early in order to get one of the steps to sit on. The heat was stifling. The windows were closed for the sun and only a chink, opened for air, allowed a bit of light to lay on the sill. I half-closed my eyes and looked at the light through the stained glass of the window trying to see it, now only through the yellow dress of a saint, now through the blue veil of another, now through a pink face. I remember that old man, delicately picking his way among us before the service began, with something of affectionate strangeness. He was the only white man who was not a sailor or a priest that I had been so close to. Sometimes, as he passed, I reached a hand stealthily out and touched his trousers.

When he died, and your mother insisted that we go to his funeral, as if he were a priest, I wondered, holding your hand (I was responsible for you then), who would be playing the organ at his funeral. It was Lafond. For years afterwards he walked among us as the old man had done, on his way to the choir loft. And, for all those years, his brown skin had intimidated me, intimidated me in a way that the skin of his successor, who looks like you and me, never would have.

Years later, sitting in one of the pews reserved for college boys, I remembered that frail white man and Lafond every feast day. I had exchanged one discomfort for another. I had given up the steps leading to the choir loft, which my mother still used, and the hour's advance to get a seat on one of them. I now wore grey flannel trousers, school blazer, and a tie in the crowded church. But I had a pew to go to. I would sit in it, with the other college boys, and laugh when, across the aisle, someone who had come early to get a seat had to give it up to its owner. Often, even despite the arrival of the church orderly, the usurper refused for a long time to get up, and his quiet intransigence gave us even greater pleasure. For we knew that, in the end, he would get up to walk shamefacedly, the more so the longer he had refused to get up, towards the back of the church.

I could afford to laugh. I was safe. Your mother was on the steps leading to the choir loft. Nobody would eject her from there. But it was always with regret that I watched the usurper get up and walk away. I wanted him to continue to be defiant, to refuse absolutely to move. I wanted to see him carried bodily out of the pew by the church orderlies, perhaps be clubbed by the truncheons they carried and which I had never seen them use. For I knew, sitting in the pews reserved for us, that I, like him, was a usurper, and it was my own defiance that I wished had been total. It was myself that I watched going shamefacedly down the aisle.

I was always disappointed. No matter how long he remained obdurately sitting in the pew, the usurper always got up in the end and walked sheepishly away. And, always, it was myself that I watched self-justifiedly taking the place he had vacated for me. I knew that, in a few years, I would insist, even more forcibly than those I observed, that every usurper remove himself to make room for me.

Even on days when the church was not full your mother refused to sit in another's pew. She preferred to stand at the back of the church. For she was proud, that woman, not, like your father, for others to see, but inside, steelily. And, obviously, she had known her place. I remember a remark I heard her make one day when she and one of her friends were talking about a man who had struck a priest.

I remember how impossible that had seemed. His cassock, even more than the colour of his skin, had always placed the priest in the area of my utmost respect and of my fear. I could not imagine a priest being hit. Nor could my mother. She repeated the words *"vieux negre"* many times, with exasperation and with disdain. Had it been your father, I should not have paid too much attention to his use of those words. But your mother did not use them often. The man she used them to describe was, clearly, beneath her contempt.

Arguing with the priest, he had wanted to know why he had to go to confession before he could be allowed to be godfather to his best friend's child. My mother, speaking about it, was appalled. He even told the priest, went so far, my mother said heatedly in patois to her friend, as to tell the priest that he did not see why his best friend's child had to be baptized on a special day because its father and mother were not married. My mother used words like "show-off" and "stupid". She was intolerantly angry. She called the man "wharf-rat". And she used the word to describe, disdainfully, one who did not, as she did hers, know his place. I try, as I write this, to imagine the surprise of the priest whose authority could never have prepared him for the explosion of the man's violence. I cannot imagine it. The whole thing, even now, is still too improbable. I see consternation only on the faces of those who wait, patiently and properly, for the illegitimate children they are godparents to, to be baptized. One of them leads the violent man away. All are shocked by the explosion of language and action within the church. I try to see the incident as if it happened before my eyes, and the angry and defiant man, leaving the church, had brushed against me as he passed. It seems I can hear him muttering angrily under his breath. I hear your mother say, as if to atone for the blow the priest had just received:

"Me, hit a priest? Even if he had slapped me, I was going to turn my face for him to slap again. Much less for me to hit him at all."

But, more clearly, I remember the vehement protestation of allegiance from her friend. Holding the cup she sipped her coffee from – it was morning and I had just come from Mass – she had sucked her teeth disdainfully and proclaimed that if any priest had slapped her she would not only give her cheek for him to slap again but would turn her arse – she used the most vulgar patois equivalent of the word – for him to kick. My mother sent me out of the room. But it was too late. I can still see that black and ample market vendor with the dirty apron before her swing excitedly around as she had spoken and the splashes of coffee that had spilled on to the floor.

Through the open window of the room I went to sunlight poured. It struck the large bottle of pepper sauce. Seen through the yellow mixture of ground pepper, tumeric and mustard, it reminded me of the light coming through the stained-glass window of the church. I remember the steps leading to the choir loft and the frail, white organist picking his way delicately among us as though there is a connection between him and that excited and voluminous woman turning spiritedly around to allow a priest to kick her in the arse…

I had often wished to enter the Social Club. The mob, although it could still hear the music you made and the sound of your feet stomping on the veranda of the club above it, was no longer dancing. The men and women milled about the Club entrance like animals after a long drive, content to wait on the street for you to come out again. I overcame my antipathy. It was my first opportunity to enter the Club. Neither the sweaty crowd I would have to go through, nor the opinion I had so much hoped to establish among those I imagined watched me from their verandas, was strong enough to prevent me from taking it. I crossed the street, went through the waiting mass, and climbed up the stairs. The uniformed stewards at the top of them made no attempt to stop me.

I recognized the Club at once. I had seen it before: the tables and chairs on the veranda; the wrought-iron railings that allowed one to look down on to the street; the shelves with the bottles of liquor; the green-topped billiard table illuminated by lights under a huge hanging reflector; the white-tunicked stewards with the green braid down the seams of their trousers and on the cuffs of their jackets. I might have been, but for the noise you and your friends were making, and the distress of the stewards at the head of the stairs, in that other Club which, before it had been rebuilt out of town, I had often observed. From the gym (I went to it, not to work out, but to observe those who did and secretly compare their bodies with mine) I had looked through the jalousies of the always closed windows at white men leaning over their green-topped billiard table and lounging on the veranda over drinks that tunicked, black men served them. I was disappointed. The Social Club was so familiar! I knew it intimately, just as I knew the space between the altar and the altar rails, without ever having set foot in it. I did not remain.

About to go down the stairs again I saw one or two of the crowd who had sneaked up with you and were dancing, unseen by the stewards who guarded the stairs. I resented their presence. I felt they were out of their place. I was satisfied, moving through the waiting crowd that waited patiently outside, that they should wait. The stewards had not stopped me from entering the Club. And it seemed I had always been able to climb those stairs and sit down in one of the chairs on the veranda. It gave me pleasure and satisfaction to see so many people milling about the Club entrance because they were not allowed to enter. I looked towards the Square. The verandas were all empty. The crowd continued to wait patiently on the street. It still knew its place. But I was sorry. For now there was no one standing on a veranda to see how quickly I had come down again from the Club.

PAUL

The other day, in one of my books, I came across a picture of myself. For years, while you lived in that room, and after you went away, while Phyllis occupied it, I had not looked at those books. For more than eight years, then, they had lain untouched on the bookshelf that I had had made of the same expensive wood as the desk. But, coming again into the room to write, I saw them every night. The memory of the long hours I had spent with them, which seemed so useless now, mocked me. I decided to throw them away. I had no more use for, nor need of them.

And then, one night, prompted by a mood, I took up one of them. I did not choose. I had come in as usual to write to you. The bookshelf was behind my chair. Almost as if I were afraid, and looking in front of me, I put a hand back and pulled out a book. It was a book of Apologetics. There was an inscription on the front page in writing I barely recognized as my own. The inscription was contained between inverted commas. "If any protestant wants to argue your religion with you, tell them you never argue religion. In that way you will always be safe." The inverted commas suggested a quote but I could no longer remember whom it was I had quoted nor why I should have considered the statement important enough for me to copy it down on the front page of my book. Eager always for guidelines, I must obviously have considered this advice useful and worth remembering. The word "your" was underlined. I read that quotation over and over trying to go beyond the handwriting I barely recognized to the person I was who had written the inscription. It was difficult. I could only see an anonymous woolly head in a class listening to the tall, white-robed Irishman who, for half an hour every morning, taught us sixth-formers Apologetics. I remembered Skeete.

Long before that time he and I had been friends. He was an Anglican, and I, a Roman Catholic; and each of us knew that his religion was better than that of the other. We argued ceaselessly about religion. I had liked Skeete. We both had the same ambition. We were both preparing to take the scholarship examination. We talked about what we should do when we went to college and after we had left it. Skeete was going to become a lawyer. And he would pass a law forbidding people to walk about the streets selling sweets. His mother, walking with the sweets she had made in little heaps on a wooden tray she carried on her head, and in her hand a box, for her to sit on at a bus-stop or outside a school at recreation time, embarrassed him. He did not tell me so. But, hearing the one law he always insisted he should enact once he became a lawyer, I understood. We spoke about previous scholarship winners and of how many had been Anglicans and how many Roman Catholics. We had little knowledge but we quarrelled fiercely about the figures each one of us produced. Our quarrels affected our friendship. Sometimes, very, very seldom, we compared what we had learned at our respective schools and attempted to teach each other. But generally, when we were to-gether, we argued most of the time.

When I won a scholarship, and he didn't, I saw it as a vindication. I was sorry for Skeete but, as a Roman Catholic, I was unable to sympathize fully with him. It was his fault for being an Anglican and having attended an Anglican school. I felt justified in my Roman Catholicism and was proud that I, too, had contributed to the Roman Catholic record of achievement on the island. Skeete had paid the penalty for being an Anglican and deserved to do so. I suggested that he might have passed the examination if he had been to our – I am sure I must have used the possessive – Roman Catholic school. For the first time he did not argue with me. He shook his head quietly; but it was not to contradict what I had said. He looked solemn. It had been his only chance at the scholarship examination. The next year he would be too old. He passed the back of his hand against his mouth. The familiar gesture made him look helpless. Perhaps he, too, was thinking that we might have argued less and worked together more. After that we did not argue. But it was not so much because he or I had changed. He went to work on a schooner, I went to college. In time we ceased to speak to each other.

I read the inscription again and wondered, this time, what part Skeete might have played in making me write it down on the front page of my book five or six years after our last argument. And I was sitting in the room, thinking about Skeete and turning idly the pages of the book, when I saw the picture. It surprised me. In an unpleasant way. I had forgotten how well I used to look. Even with the woollen sweater on you could see the quality of my form. My chest was like a box. There was strength and vigour in the lean face that smiled back at me. There had been determination in that chin. I felt pain.

I had forgotten about the picture. I had taken it on another island to which I had gone as a member of the school cricket team. Your father had not wished to let me go. He said it cost too much money. Your mother pleaded on my behalf and, grumbling, your father allowed me to go. I remember us crowded on the deck of the small motor-vessel that took us in one night to the other island. The next morning it lay before us. I felt strange and excited. I had not looked at town and its background of hills from the sea before. From the town I had looked at the hills on one hand and at the sea on the other. From the hills I had looked down to the town and at the sea beyond it. Looking over the side of the motor-vessel, waiting for the rowing-boats to take us ashore, I felt I was beginning something new and meaningful.

I was not wrong. More even than this initial strangeness was the strangeness of the entire interlude. I was – we all were – served at table. Maids made up our beds. Everywhere we went we wore our uniform – grey flannel trousers, white shirts, school blazer with crest, blue tie. It was having to provide a new uniform that your father had objected to. It was the uniform which I was most thankful for. Among us, on that island, the distinguishing marks I knew at home were absent. We existed for the islanders without antecedent to characterize us. No one on that island knew where I lived on mine. We went to the same parties, had lunch with the Governor, were entertained in homes the equivalent of which I had never entered on our island.

And I was a success. I scored a century in my first match. The picture had been taken soon after that. I don't remember the photographer. He was a schoolboy

I had impressed who wished to be my friend. He was obviously well-to-do. I never saw him again. I had wanted the picture to be more than the simple record of the successful athlete. I wanted to preserve in it something of the new social atmosphere I moved in. My rich friend carried a woollen sweater in his hand. I do not know why, since he was not a player, except that it was expensive and therefore difficult to own. My school blazer, of which I was so proud, seemed ordinary to me. I asked my new friend to lend me his sweater. Then I wiped my forehead. I remembered that in pictures of me that had appeared in the papers on my island, after I had played a long innings, the sun was always like an explosion on my black, greasy forehead.

I must have felt that I succeeded in capturing the social atmosphere I had wanted. Why else should I have kept this picture? There is no other picture of me in this house – neither as successful athlete nor successful student.

We spent a glorious three weeks on the island. Then we came back home. I put away the school uniform. It was to be used now only on Sundays and on special school occasions. Once more, I ate fried fish and bread and drank hot cocoa for breakfast and dinner. I served myself at lunch. Your father said nothing about my performance, showed no interest in the bat I brought back as a prize. Your mother, happy to see me back, was glad I had enjoyed the trip. There was nothing to be done, no parties to attend, no games to prepare for or to go to. The last days of the holidays seemed to drag. One afternoon, walking past the clean fronts of the houses on the edge of Columbus Square, on my way to read the foreign periodicals in the library, I saw Patricia and two other girls walking home from work. No one in the street, filled with clerks, civil servants and other people going home from their jobs, seemed to know me. It was windy. Patricia's frock began to rise. She laughed and held it down with her hands. I saw her thighs. She and her friends, talking animatedly to one another, went by. They had not noticed me looking at them. I went on past the shaded as yet unpeopled verandas and entered the library.

It is out of such small beginnings that the big things come. Patsy, laughing and holding down her dress in the wind, had seemed accessible and familiar. We had not spoken to each other since she and her mother had left the street we lived on to live on the other side of the river. But I knew Patsy. I did not know the other girls. I knew few other girls. I had had little time for girls. I had not wished to talk to those I could approach easily and had been afraid to talk to the others. But I had met and talked with girls on that island where I had been a success and where servants had served, and new, rich friends courted me. Patsy, walking happily that day before the clean fronts of the houses, had been something I recognized and knew I could get close to. I reached for her out of my renewed ordinariness.

It was like a selection. I began to see her on the streets, in the store where she worked, among the crowd that watched the school play. I did not look out for her. And, at first, I did not speak to her. On the island life was returning to normal. But I could not forget what I had been exposed to on the other one. When I ate at home, I remembered the meals people had served me with. When I walked the streets in my ordinary clothes, I remembered the uniform that had marked me out for the islanders and had eliminated the difference between me and the other members of the team. I remembered the bathrooms when I bathed in the yard and poured water over myself from the baignoire with a calabash. I was dissatisfied and angry. And Patsy, poor girl, was the person I chose to vent my frustration and anger upon.

I have used the word "selection". I write "chose" now. At the time, I was not aware I had made a choice. Patsy, I have said, was both recognizable and accessible. I did not fear to approach her. She did not threaten me. I feared no rebuff from her. I understand only now how low, in reality, the level of my confidence had been. Not all my triumphs, on the sports field or in the classroom, had raised it. One day, returning late from the playing-fields, I met Patricia. The street lights were already on and for long stretches between them, on that poorly lit street where she lived, it was comfortably dark. I walked her home.

And yet the desolation that followed my return from that island was not new. It had been merely more intense. For years, after my public triumphs on the playing-fields, I had been returning to silence within our home. Your mother was always too busy. Your father pretended lack of interest. Neither of them had ever come to the playing-fields to see me. I understand why he never referred to the glowing, overwritten reports in the newspapers. Success at sports was not at the centre of his scheme for our achievement and, even though he must have derived pleasure and satisfaction from our reputation, he could not encourage us to be sportsmen. I understand that. But can it explain why I cannot remember one word from him about my good performances? Always, it was my failures alone he commented upon and seemed to respond to. I can hear him say even now, "I see you scored a duck again", or, "I hear you threw away another goal", as if I were just another worthless son who had disgraced his father. I learned, in time, not to take his pretended indifference too seriously. But do you understand now why the acclaim of the public had always been so important for me, why I pretended it was not, and why I worked secretly so hard to receive it?

On that island from which I had just returned, my relationship with my admirers, for the first time, had not been defined only in terms of their acclamation which I pretended not to care for. For the first time, I had moved freely within a circle that I had not felt, as your father had felt with the one he moved in, compelled to repudiate. I had been comfortable within it and had desired, and been gratified by, the expressions of its admiration. I had not pretended indifference at the parties I attended when I was complimented on my performance. I expected, looked forward to, and was delighted to receive those compliments from people with whom I knew I belonged. Those compliments were not the general roar of a public at large. They were the comments on my excellence made by the members of a group I was a part of. When I came back home it was normal that my father should be silent. But the events on that island had been unusual for me, and your father's usual silence had been more than ever difficult for me to acknowledge.

You alone knew how hard I worked for the admiration I pretended I did not care for. Your father assumed that my intense practising in the yard was normal. You knew it was abnormal and an exaggeration. But could it have been otherwise? Your father had no experience of his own to measure ours against. He could not assess ability since he had no conception of what constituted it nor of how it should be measured. There were no pictures of himself standing with other boys in a school uniform, none of himself on cricket or football teams.

72

And out of his experience alone he could find little or no advice to pass on to us. Perhaps that is why he left us so much alone as we grew older. His notions of success and failure could only be based on standards that were not his own. And, for him, it was the public response to my performance that became the determinant. But neither he, nor the public, had the knowledge which made all performance relative. For me to appear to fail, therefore, no matter what the circumstances, was always to incur his and the public's disapproval, and his sarcastic comments in the house. How could I not, in the end, repudiate him?

With my son it was to be different. We should have a common experience. I would show him clippings, photographs and certificates. I would refer him to standards I had known and had myself tested. We would communicate. His mother, laughing, would contradict my too-elaborate boasts.

Patsy could not have been that mother. And Michael was not that son. Michael was only the very badly cracked image of the son I might have had. I could not bear to look at him. The vision of that son, whose place he usurped, had been too complete, even though it, too, like my intense practising in the yard, had been an exaggeration. That is why I neglected him. Both of us, my son and I, appeared to me only as travesty and an imperfect imitation. I found it intolerable to look at us. He reminded me too much of what I felt I had been to your father and I feared that, in time, I too might be to him what your father had been to us. I had had enough, already, of sacrifice and expectation. I remembered your father's anxiety and refused to be made anxious. If you had not taken him with you, Michael might have become carpenter or fisherman and I should not have cared. For I was unwilling to depend on Michael's future achievement as your father had depended on yours and mine; and I preferred to do nothing that might resemble, even remotely, the kind of contract with my son that your father had felt compelled to make with you and with me.

How can I talk to you about Patsy? I feel that, married to Phyllis, you understand. Perhaps it is my defence. I shall not talk about her. But there is that Christmas day and the events that took place on it and I will tell you about them. I had been out of school for three months and teaching at the college. You will remember me clearly of that time. I bullied you constantly in class, asked you questions the answers to which you could not know, punished you for the least offence. I did not realize that I was being to you what your father had been to us. Or that my behaviour was the result of my own confusion and lack of confidence. I had chosen you to illustrate my excellence as teacher and disciplinarian, you particularly, because you were my brother and no one, I felt, therefore, could question my performance. You resented this and complained at home. But you should have known our father could only have approved of my severity. Like him, I had confused roles. I insisted that you call me Mr. Breville at home just as you and the other boys called me Mr Breville at school. Or Sir. I carried into the classrooms resentments and quarrels that had had their origin at home. And, caught between the home and the classroom, you could not escape. Relations between us, never strong, broke down completely.

I did not care. My position was unassailable at home and in the school. Your father had begun to be friendly to me. In my quarrels with you he was inevitably on my side. At school, for the purposes of discipline, no teacher ever was wrong. I was out of reach, of yours and, it seemed to me, of anybody's. Examination results had come in from England that day. I had done absolutely well. There was talk of a First. As usual I pretended indifference and lack of interest. Earlier, I had seen Patricia pass on the street. No one, I told myself, knew about us. The thought elated me. Now she was in the house and I could hear her talking in patois to my mother. She had come, she said, because it was Christmas and she had not seen my parents for such a long time. There was no talk about me and she and I did not speak to each other. Her new dress seemed too colourful, her lips too red, the stockings she wore pretentious. But her firm, well-shaped body invited me. I felt myself become erect as she prattled to my mother and sipped falernum.

Outside, there was a band of masqueraders. Your father was looking at them from the window. I heard the sound of flute and drum. I joined him and we looked out at the dancers together. I was thinking how successfully Patsy and I were fooling everybody else. I heard her say goodbye to my mother. It seemed her voice, which I could hear distinctly above the noise made by the masqueraders, contained in it a message for me. Your father, his pipe still in his mouth, grunted goodbye without turning away from the dancers. I said nothing and did not turn to look at her.

The band performing outside was a band of fishermen. I recognized one or two of the uncostumed musicians. I tried to make out the other dancers behind their masks. I could smell Patsy's perfume. It was new. Obviously she had bought it for the holiday. I did not like it. I had not made out the dancers. I became more determined to find out who they were. I decided to go outside so as to get closer to them. I turned, and Patsy's cheap perfume was strong in the room. I became erect again. Outside, I saw her walking by herself in the sun, moving away from the dancers, her pink umbrella closed, and the sun dancing, as she walked, on her too-greased, half-Indian, half-Negroid hair. Her body, and my memory of it, was more than a counterbalance, in terms of arousal and of remembered and anticipated pleasure, for the shame looking at her caused me to feel.

I had no difficulty in making my way to the inner edge of the circle of onlookers within which the masqueraders were dancing. No one objected to my shoving. Someone, tipsy, patted my shoulder with sufficient familiarity for me to resent the gesture and said loudly, "Eh, eh, look Mr. Footballer-in-chief. Give the Mr. room to pass." And he made a path for me. Soon I was standing on the edge of the dancing area. The flute music was as agile as monkeys. The drumming was a writhing, furious background. I tried to make out the dancers by looking through the big eyeholes of their masks which fitted loosely. I was looking for a fraction of movement to recognize, a gait I remembered, the drop of a shoulder or the carriage of a head – something I had seen before which might serve as an indication now. I looked closely at the dancers. I could make out not one of them.

The pennies fell. A man, uncostumed like the musicians, moved among the dancers and collected the coins. Every now and then one of the dancers was singled out and a coin was sent specifically to him. He caught it. Then whirled his appreciation enthusiastically. If the coin fell on the ground, he left it alone. The drumming and flute music increased in tempo. The dancing became more frenzied. I could not hope to make out the dancers now. I gave up my attempts at recognition and tried, instead, to determine which of the costumed masqueraders performed the best.

The coins were falling thick and fast. The drumming and the flute music had become even more intense. The dancers' gyrations assumed a frenzy that even I found hypnotic. Their bodily contortions matched the increased and seemingly ever increasing tempo of the music. The onlookers, absorbed, were quiet.

But there was a dancer who hardly danced. I had noticed no coin thrown to him. Once or twice I had seen a colleague, popular with the crowd, pass a coin he had caught over to his friend who seemed either to be tired or to have hurt himself. It seemed a form of encouragement. And, paying more and more attention to him, and less and less to his accomplished colleagues, I decided that he was a beginner. I watched him. He hardly moved. Then someone called out. All the dancers, eager to have their merit indicated by the thrown coin, looked up. It was your father, smoking his pipe and unsmiling, who had called. He was pointing to my incompetent friend. The music seemed to increase in tempo. Two of the other dancers whirled joyfully, exuberantly about him. Then moved away. Your father threw him a coin. The dancer caught it. He began to move a little more. Your father threw him another coin. Then another. And another. The dancer caught them. He began to gyrate. He leaped into the air, opened his legs, spread his arms. Bending forward at the waist, he shook his entire body as if he suffered an extraordinary fit. His exaggerated performance was ungraceful and inelegant. Another coin from your father hit his back and rolled away. He paid no attention to it. The flute and drumming sounded maddeningly. The other dancers were hardly dancing now. I could not see their expressions behind their masks. Your father, about to throw another coin, was laughing now. He threw it and it lodged, by accident, in the dancer's belt. The crowd roared. All the onlookers shouted and clapped their hands. The other dancers came to life again. One of the onlookers, a fisherman too, ran across the open space, a bottle of rum in his hand, and patted the dancer approvingly on his back. There were shouts and whistles. Even the children were yelling now. The spell cast by the intensely beautiful dancing of the other masqueraders was broken. I turned and walked disgustedly away.

I did not want to go back to the house. I did not want to see your father just now. I walked the sunny streets filled with people. The sounds from the music of several bands, conflicting with one another, reverberated inharmoniously. A band was approaching me. The dancers moved ahead of the musicians, lithe and active. Bits of glass, attached to their dresses, reflected the sun. Paper streamers trailed colourfully in the breeze behind their elaborate headgear. They came nearer and their music prevailed. Flute and drum became orderly again after the brief and frenzied inharmony. It lasted only a short time. As the band moved on, its music was lost again in the chaos of conflicting sounds. Suddenly it seemed to me that a hundred different bands were playing their music in the small town, and I wanted to get away from the noise they made. Then I saw that one of the dancers had come and had started to dance before me.

I did not give him the customary coin. Nor did I smile and move away. I was no longer in a mood for masqueraders, nor for those who threw coins to them. The dancer followed me across the street, not paying any attention to my mood. All about me now there was the general inharmony of flute and drum. I tried to move on. The dancer impeded my progress. I turned to move to the left. He placed himself before me, jigging up and down, his cupped hand held before him. I could see the sweat under his armpits and smell rum on his breath. My decision to give him nothing hardened. I turned to the right. He was jigging in front of me. I turned completely about. He was in front of me. I could see the reddened eyes behind the eyeholes of his mask. The streamers in his headpiece rustled disagreeably. I was becoming annoyed. His insistence and refusal to acknowledge my mood angered me. More and more people had stopped to look at us. I turned about again. He was there, posturing before me. I smiled. I whispered fiercely, "Why the fuck don't you leave me alone."

The vehemence of the expression, so alien to the spirit of the game he had been playing, took him by surprise. For a second he seemed to stand absolutely still. His reddened eyes seemed to dilate behind the holes in his mask. Then immediately he was all movement again. He danced a little half-hearted jig. Then he ran off, the streamers of his headpiece flying behind him, to join his friends.

I had no feeling of triumph. It seemed, immediately, that I had been as cruel as your father had been, throwing the coins and laughing. I crossed the street again to walk before the rum-shops and in the shade before them. People were noisy before counters. A radiogram sounded loudly. I felt irritated and dissatisfied. Then I saw Patricia. She was talking to another girl. Instantly I was erect again. I stood where she could not help but see me and waited for a while. I had always avoided talking to her on the streets. But very quickly I was tired of waiting and went up to her. I said something about the parcel she had left at home. She understood: I could see her following me a few minutes later. Once more I crossed to the other side of the street. From there, without too obviously turning to look at her, I could see her on the opposite pavement walking a little way behind me. Every now and then, out of the corner of an eye, I caught sight of her pink umbrella rolled up in spite of the sun.

My mood, made up of irritation and disgust, was now enhanced by a feeling of power. The promptness of Patricia's response had helped to define that power for me. It seemed to me, walking along the noisy street and keeping a discreet eye on the pink umbrella, that I was doing something dangerous and doing it well. I began to have again, but without the elation, the feeling of confidence I had had earlier. I was superior to the masquaraders, to those who watched them perform, to the drunkards before the rum-shops. A wave of intolerance passed over me. And it included that pink umbrella as well. I decided, suddenly, to end our secret affair. The pink umbrella, the glint of the sun on over-oiled hair, the stockings – all were a part of that of which I was so intolerant, and, at that moment, felt so superior to. They were, all of them, objects of my contempt.

I walked, followed by Patricia, out of the reach of flute and drum to the very edge of the town. Then I took the winding, up-and-down hill road to the beach. It was empty. Patsy and I disappeared under the almond and coconuts. I could hear the sounds of trampled leaves and of snapping dried branches as she followed me. We were well within the brush when I turned to look at her.

There was neither joy nor expectation on her face. She was breathing hard. Without a word I began to undress her. She said nothing. Her dress was wet in the upper back and under the armpits. I removed her petticoat, her bra, her pants. I could see she was amazed, possibly frightened. I had not had her naked before. But she did not say a word. I took off her stockings. There were now runs in them. I could sense her uneasiness which, however, did not bother me. I felt, at the same time, that Patricia trusted me completely. I undressed and we lay on my trousers on the ground.

It was ridiculously short. And immediately I wanted to put on my clothes and walk back alone to the town. I said nothing to her. What could I say? She had not complained, had said nothing. But my physical insufficiency, the sorry lack of containment, made me feel inadequate. And my inadequacy, after the feeling of confidence and superiority, and my intolerance in the town, depressed me. I was still within her when I said, "We'll have to stop this."

I knew that there would be no response, no complaint, no plea. It had always been like this. Patricia had never spoken easily to me. At least not after I had begun to make fun of her pronunciation and the patois expressions she transliterated when she tried to speak to me in English. Her inarticulateness pleased me. It saved time and prevented many things from coming between us. It had always been her body only that I wanted.

I moved out of her and sat up. She got up from my trousers and put on her petticoat. Then her stockings. Then her pants. I sat on my heels and watched her. When she was dressed and held the pink umbrella again in her hand, she looked at me. I knew that I deserved more than that pink umbrella and the too-oiled hair. I said, "You go. I think I want to stay here for a while."

I remained alone in the brush, afraid to move, long after I had ceased to hear the sounds of her going. When I got back to the town, the street lights were on. The masqueraders had gone home. The town was quiet. Only an occasional firecracker exploded. And before the rum-shops lay the drunks.

In the house your father was happy. He and some friends were drinking. I knew immediately that something extraordinary had happened. The note had been delivered personally by one of the Brothers even though it was Christmas day. Your father told me so, giving it to me to read. I had had a First. I had topped my class. Your father's friendliness and congratulations were strange to me. I wished he had been his usual non-commenting self. His friends stood smiling, a little ill at ease, it seemed to me. Then they shook my hand. Your father was laughing and talking. I had never seen him like this before. It was clear that this was the achievement that he had been working and waiting for and had all along seen very clearly. I was on the threshold of his success. The note was back on the table where I had put it. For once, genuinely, I was indifferent to news of my success. I looked at your father. His face reminded me of the dancer's exaggerations and of his coins, my father's, that had encouraged them. I said something or other. He said that your mother, hearing the news, had gone to church. I don't know why he said that. I had not asked him. I went upstairs. Three weeks later, the first time I saw Patsy again, she told me she was pregnant.

PETER & PHYLLIS

"When are you going?"

"The day after tomorrow. You and me. And Michael."

"Perhaps this time it will be better?"

"Perhaps."

"I may even be pregnant."

Peter, on the toilet seat, heard the words, his and Phyllis's, as if they had just been spoken, as clearly as those other words which she had uttered earlier that night, lying beneath him, and which he had tried to stifle with a hand over her mouth:

"Peter, I love you. I love you, Peter."

Her acceptance of his offer for her to come and live with him again had been like a coin falling into a slot that had waited for it for eight years. For the next few days she prepared quietly to leave their island to which he had returned from the metropolis he had loved and studied in. And when the two of them moved to the bungalow on the campus, it was as if, for all the eight years of their separation, while she lived with his parents, she had been preparing to make this journey to another island to set up house with him; as if the house they moved into had been her father's and, long ago, through years of child-hood occupation, she had grown familiar with, and known intimately, all the rooms it contained. Happy and contented, she had moved through those rooms as though they were an inheritance. At the end of six months, even though he had begun to have doubts about his usefulness at the university, he was relaxed with Phyllis and as contented as a dog in the house. And after a year his relationship with her provided the only protection against the increasing questioning of his motives for holding on to his appointment at the university.

Because he doubted more and more the meaningfulness of what he had studied abroad and had returned to teach now, and his job, increasingly, seemed merely a means of providing security for himself and his family, coming home to Phyllis was like coming to what his real purpose in life was – to make Phyllis happy. When they were together in the house, he wished that the purpose of his life, and his only responsibility, could be to make her as happy as he could, for his own sake and because she deserved to be. He wanted his world, and Phyllis's, to exist by itself, closed and apart from the one about them. But the possibility of their happiness seemed to depend on his own first and on his satisfaction with himself as a member of the community he had returned to live in. And with himself and the role he played in it he was becoming increasingly unhappy and dissatisfied.

He tried to explain to Phyllis. But she was not interested. She seemed unwilling to take his doubts seriously. "If only I had the education you have," she used to say to him. And, despite his growing dissatisfaction, he understood. He knew, as she did, what the education he had received, no matter how much, now, he thought of it as irrelevant, had made possible for him. And what it would have meant for her. After her father had died, and she had been forced to leave school, she came back from her job as counter clerk to turn over the pages of his school

84

books on afternoons and to talk of going back to school as if she believed what she said.

He discovered now that she was impatient with ideas and unwilling, or unable, to deal with them. She was comfortable only when she talked of things she had seen or heard or events that had happened to her or that she anticipated. She left her sentences unfinished, used exclamation and gesture more than the word. Her language was the language of a child, or of a slave to whom language had not been taught. When she spoke patois, she used English words; and the English she used was little more than transliterations of words and phrases from patois. More than a century after Emancipation her language was still a makeshift one used not so much to express as to indicate.

So he had brought her books to read. She had not wished to offend him and had pretended interest. At night she sat at the table, a book open before her, a dictionary, open too, next to it. Peter suddenly would raise his head from the book he read or the essay he corrected to find that she was asleep. Sometimes he left her alone. At others, confused by sentiments of sympathy and disappointment, he would shake her gently and, instantly, she was awake and smiling to show how awake she had always been. Laughing, she protested that she had not really been asleep. He watched her take up the book again and, for a brief moment, the lighted room (and themselves within it) was like a haven against the questioning of the worth of what he did and against the feeling of irrelevance and chaos which overwhelmed him every time he stepped out of the house. And he used to think: to make her happy, to be able to spend the rest of my life making her happy…

But if he was tired or particularly despondent after a

class, her language or any instance of her unwillingness to think for herself irritated him extremely. Then her lack of interest in the books he brought her and in anything that did not concern the two of them, or those immediately connected with them, assumed the status of symbol, became the sign of her singlemindedness and determination in a context he had remembered less and less but which, surging in his memory, seemed to indicate how cunningly she had induced him into marrying her. For, even after a year of their renewed togetherness, the memory of that possibility of her cunning, so active and poisonous during his affair with Anna in the metropolis, still lay, like a snake asleep, curled up in a corner within him.

Yet their relationship, renewed, had progressed beyond friendship. Her confidence and assurance in the beginning had known no bounds. If he came back early from a party – she preferred to remain alone at home – she asked laughingly which devil he feared would take her away. She had laughed at the picture of Daphne, the plump, white girl he had lived with after Anna had left him. And, looking at the picture he carried of Anna, she had asked whether she, Anna, always dressed as extravagantly. Neither the occasional note from Daphne he had continued to receive well into that first year, nor the bundle of Anna's notes to him, which he had kept, had seemed to arouse her jealousy. She had been like a stream flowing through well-defined banks that, over centuries, it had cut out for itself.

Her energy had seemed to exist merely to serve him with. If he left his shoes in the sitting-room, she removed them. If he forgot his shirt on the back of a chair on a hot afternoon, she took it away. He dropped an ashtray, and she was there to pick up the ashes and cigarette butts. He recognized her devotion. And her efficiency. Meals were always on time. She seemed to have no other pleasure than to take care of him, the house, and to be comfortable with him in it. If she was in the kitchen and he was in the sitting-room, she kept the door between the rooms open. She came into the bathroom while he bathed to talk to him. She was with him sometimes while he sat on the toilet. She made him feel the centre of her world. And a fraud.

Coming home from work, he saw her standing at the open door, smiling and waiting for him. At other times, just as he placed his hand on the knob, the door opened inward and Phyllis was there, standing before it and smiling conspiratorially at him. And he would smile too, the memory of the past, stirred by a growing dissatisfaction with Phyllis, qualifying, and lending to his smile, a quiet that was beginning to be distance. She treated him as though he had been engaged in the most important and strenuous of activities. She told him often, "You must be tired." Her exaggerated opinion of the worth and exacting nature of his work contained for him a sarcasm she had not intended. In time he no longer tried to show her she was mistaken. The importance of his work continued to exist for her and less and less for him. His dissatisfaction and his disenchantment grew and he began to regret again, and resent, each time a little more, her intellectual failings.

Her complexion and her hair, once, when he and Phyllis had lived near the market, long before there had been the possibility of marriage between them, had made a promise to him. He had taken much pleasure in the name she bore – her father's name, the well-known and respected name of a white islander, estate owner, Oxford graduate, and lawyer who had never bothered, because he did not need to, to practise his profession on the island. Even the new insecurity after her father's death and the desperate (and often seedy) fight by her mother for survival had not dimmed his delight in Phyllis's complexion. The lightness of her skin and the quality of her mulatto hair had been compensation for their forced marriage which he had resented. But now the assets of complexion and long hair lost their value and he regretted once more, and without any compensation this time, his marriage to her.

He thought of Anna more and more, forgetting the human qualities he knew (now) she lacked, imagining her support. He saw the two of them together and using the training they had received in the metropolis, not to secure a good living within the serpent's head of privilege that others had created before them, but to investigate conditions at home that for too long had been uninvestigated and had acquired the right of custom and of law. And, so deep had his need become, he forgot the Anna he had known in the metropolis, the intensely black girl with straightened hair who avoided metropolitan immigrant areas because she had not been like the immigrants at home and would have nothing to do with them in the city, who frequented the concert halls because she had been brought up on classical music and played superbly the piano, who hated white people for their condescension but resented even more the immigrants "who gave those people so much to say about us". In the end she had avoided her white friends completely, refusing, as she explained to him, "to be cause for their self-righteousness". And she had avoided her black friends as well. "I am an individual," she announced more than once, "a person. Not a bit of blackness."

In the final months of their relationship Anna had

been confused and disintegrating. Her nervousness had increased, her impatience become stronger, her intolerance of black uneducated and white in general more marked. More than ever he had felt himself the pole she quietly draped herself around, when they were alone together, but from which, leaving him, she unfolded, driven by the breeze of an increasing alienation, to flap her individual brilliance for all others, black and white alike, to hear and to see. Though she had not wished to show her increased dependency, she called on him more and more, spoke to him on the telephone for longer and longer hours, remained in his room, stretched out on the bed, talking, talking, always talking, for hours, her expensive coat lying on the bed beside her. She pretended impatience with his non-intellectual advances, rejected his little touches on her short, straightened hair, played down his compliments on her elegance without ever being inelegant, even when she lay on the bed next to her coat, chided him for not being serious when she would be and for wanting to pretend that he was what he was no longer and, after the education he had received, would never again become.

And more than once – in his room, in hers, at a restaurant she had taken him to – he had felt her gaze, like that of a small animal standing upwind to smell him, as though her eyes were fingers within a second-hand establishment poking surreptitiously for quality.

She had been like a colourful bird flying frantically in a closed room and he had been too busy admiring the effect created by its beating wings to notice the distress they signalled. Phyllis, before their quarrels, satisfied and contented, had seemed not to understand the nature of his own distress. Or even that he was distressed.

She seemed more and more like a child to him, to be

protected, played with, made happy. But she was not a child and his previous affection for her, becoming more and more condescending, like that of an adult for a child, contained in it now something of the unpleasant and unsatisfying. She knew the ratings of the ten most popular songs in England and in America, and she listened to the songs daily on the local radio programmes. But news of riots, race riots, in America, events in Africa, what happened to the immigrants, of which her brother was one, in England, seemed not to interest her. The murder of a couple on a deserted beach at night where they were making love in their parked car frightened and preoccupied her. Many times she mentioned that she had seen strange black men loitering about. She believed, she said, they should get a dog.

But events he remembered in England, aggravated by news from America and of an increased and seemingly universal confrontation between black and white made him discern as threatening and ominous events on the island that Phyllis paid no attention to. It seemed to matter nothing to her that another foreign bank had been built, that more and more tourist "facilities" were being erected, owned by foreign companies, or that a piece of property had been sold to foreign real estate developers who advertised places in the sun in foreign magazines that never appeared locally. And recognizing, in the beautiful picture that accompanied an advertisement in a brochure, a beach she knew or mountain she had stood before, she exclaimed with pleasure.

He began to question her dependability and to regard himself as incomplete and ill-equipped with her as his wife. He had vague notions of relevant and meaningful action, something totally removed from what he was doing now, in a future that was as vague as the action he would pursue in it. He felt a need for knowledge and awareness, for himself and for all the people of the region, and Phyllis seemed not to care. He thought of the children he and Phyllis had been, untaught to question or examine, expected – trained – merely to obey and to follow in the paths of those who had walked before them, unconcerned with, and ignorant of much of what went on in the rest of the world, depending, as their parents had depended before them, on the un-questioned authority of the Church and the Law – a Church and a Law that had not been instituted for them, or by them, had not emerged from their distinc-tive needs but which, accepting blindly, they had never examined. He saw their child, his and Phyllis's, going daily with others to church, and building a dependence that would last for ever on states of guilt, on the idea of sin and punishment and self-destroying remorse; on secrecy and hypocrisy, hope and apathy, and the expec-tation of reward in another life for the hardships of this one. He could not conceive, after the child that he had been, that a child of his should be ignorant or unaware. And Phyllis, as mother of a child who was aware, he could not imagine.

The first night, and on all the other nights, that he tried to use the contraceptive, she refused to have sexual intercourse with him. He did not insist. Nor did he bother to try to explain away her confusion and her suspicions. He said he wanted time to settle down before having a child. She reminded him that he had not wished to use a contraceptive before and asked whether it was a sudden decision. They had, she said, been married for almost ten years now. She referred to her age, explained that, much as she liked Michael and wished to take care of him, he was not her child, only his brother's. He almost asked her why she was prepared to make the distinction between her child and another's when it did not seem she wanted to make the effort to prepare herself to bring up and educate the child she wanted so much to have. Lying next to her, he thought of her waiting faithfully in his parents' house for eight years.

He was struck by a quality he thought he detected that was much like arrogance in the assurance with which she had waited once before, and waited again now, for him to come to her. He began to find excuses for not coming home on afternoons after work. He spent more time in his office and swimming in the pool. Stephenson and Thea were often there. And it was there that he had met Jeannine. At night, long after Phyllis had gone to bed, he sipped rum from glasses filled with ice in the sitting-room.

One afternoon, after swimming with Stephenson and Thea and Jeannine, he took them for a drive into the hills. They came back late. Dinner in hall was over. Jeannine invited everybody for a meal. After it, Thea and Stephenson, who were preparing for examinations, left. Peter and Jeannine talked and drank alone for a long time. When he went home, he told Phyllis, who had been asleep, her head over her crossed arms, next to his meal covered with a napkin on the table, a story about a drive into the hills with Thea and Stephenson, a flat tyre and a spare tyre that itself was flat. Afterwards, it had been too late for dinner in hall and he had taken the two students to a restaurant. Phyllis said he should have brought them to the house. There was more than enough food and, besides, she had not seen Stephenson for such a long time. And that night, as if he had suddenly taken a decision not to care, he made love to her without the contraceptive. They had not made love for over five weeks.

When she told him she was pregnant and he asked her to abort, she refused. Her reasons were the same as they had been before their marriage. She was a Roman Catholic and she was afraid. They quarrelled and the past rose up again about them, surrounding him with a mist of renewed suspicion and doubt about her real motive for not aborting that first time, and of heightened shame and contempt for the young and frightened man he remembered who had married her. She told him she would not abort no matter what he did. And she asked him if he wanted to wait, as her father had waited to have her and her brothers, until he was an old man. Peter did not answer her.

In time, they ceased to discuss it. He tried, within the impositions of present time and circumstance, to make the journey all over again of his eight years away from her. He spoke to her as infrequently as he used to write and tried to render her as unreal in the house as her photograph had been in the metropolis, hidden, safely he had thought, between the pages of the book that Anna had stumbled upon.

In the beginning she did not react to his withdrawal as if, despite the nearly two years she had spent with him in the house, she had become accustomed to, and would never lose the habit of her existence in his parents' house for eight years without him. It was only when he tried to make the mental distancing physical by removing to the spare room that she rebelled. She had not complained about his silence; had merely become silent in her turn. She did not question his rejection of her in bed, had submitted uncomplainingly to his indifferent and occasional copulation. She had ceased to refer to the meals which she continued to prepare and which he did not eat, and had never referred to his refusal any longer to look at, or smile on her, or listen to what she said. He did not expect her to follow him into the spare room.

"I'm afraid to sleep alone, Peter."

He got up and walked out of the spare room. She followed him into what, until now, had been their bedroom.

"The bed is big enough. I can move to the side."

Without answering he began to move out.

"Don't go."

It was an appeal. The memory of her defiance surged. He moved on.

"Peter, I'm afraid."

He went back into the smaller room and, this time, tried to lock the door. There was no key. The keys were in the closet where they had found them. Between himself and her, the habit of locked doors and drawers had not yet begun. He sat down on the edge of the bed. She came into the room. There was a smile on her face. It was as if he had just shaken her awake again, up from the book she had fallen asleep on. When he got up and began to move past her as if to leave the room, her hold on his shirt surprised him.

"You not going nowhere."

He turned. She had not shouted. The grammatical mistake seemed to have exploded in his head. He pulled away from her and continued to walk out of the room. She held him again.

"Let me go."

"Don't go."

He began to remove the shirt she held. She transformed her hold in a flash to his trousers. And, surprised even as he did it, he hit her on the mouth and felt her hands encircle him at the waist and her body against his. He wanted to get away from her. And from himself; too, now. She held on. He pulled her face away from where it was buried in his chest and hit it again.

After that, all during her pregnancy, they quarrelled and fought.

One night, exasperated, he told her she had been cunning and deceitful and had married him to escape from the filth her parents had left her in. She fell to the floor, rigid, her eyes closed, her arms stretched out along her sides, speechless, frothing at the mouth. Terrified, unwilling to call anyone for help, he half-lifted, half-dragged her to the car. At the hospital, the doctor could not explain. The next day, sitting up in the hospital bed, she smiled at him. She looked helpless and vulnerable and he turned away from her, not smiling back. The doctor called him aside and asked what had upset her. Peter said something about bad news from home. The doctor mentioned a psychiatrist and offered to make an appointment. Peter told Phyllis nothing and did not bother with the appointment. But, driving home with Phyllis from the hospital, he found himself thinking of his father's mania for pretence and delusion, heard again the quiet English-accented voice of his brother, Paul, who had never left the island, dressed in the suit and tie that he wore, sometimes, to the dirty warehouse he worked in, and explaining that he was not really mad but only pretending to be. And it seemed, for a moment, as he drove and Phyllis sat quietly next to him, as if all the antecedents of the unborn child she carried, himself included, had manifested, in one way or another, the madness each contained within him.

Another night – she was about seven months with child then – he came home, late as usual, to find her lying on the floor of the sitting-room groaning and holding her abdomen. She told him she was having an abortion.

She had slipped on the steps as she was going down to the lawn and the pains had begun soon afterwards. Peter was instantaneously hopeful. She wanted to see a doctor. He offered to phone for one. She said she preferred to go to the hospital. She was sure she would have to go there anyhow. He asked her for the keys to the car, which for days he had been unable to find. Her answer, between groans, that she did not have them, convinced him for the first time. He thought he could get a taxi; perhaps the hospital ambulance. Grimacing with pain she shook her head. She would walk. It was not too far. She could manage. The pains did not last very long when they came. They came and went. She held her abdomen and sat up. She added that the walking would even be a good thing for her. Peter accepted what she said. Phyllis, who had fallen asleep over the books he had brought her to read, had antagonized him even more after her pregnancy, by reading book after book on childbirth and child-rearing. Groaning, she held on to his arm and stood up from the floor.

She apologized. She did not wish to bother him. But she knew he was glad for what had happened. It was what he had wanted all the time. Peter suggested the taxi again. She insisted they should walk. There was a moon, she said, they would take the short-cut through the campus, the same one he always took when he went to his woman. She smiled weakly as she said this. It would be easy. She put a hand on her abdomen and grimaced as if she were in sudden pain. Peter, happy that she was going to abort, felt she was brave and was sorry for her. He even began to think about the possibility of complications for her arising out of the abortion.

They set out. Dogs barked at them from behind fences in the shadow of huge trees which lined the edges of the pitched street they walked over. Phyllis, groaning and stopping every now and then, hung heavily on his arm. They advanced slowly, walking on their shadows in the very centre of the street. And, without speaking, they moved together over the unreal landscape of his satisfaction and his fear.

They left the area of the faculty residences, crossed the main road and came to the campus. The moon lay in a broad expanse everywhere, on the wide lawns, on the roofs and sides of buildings, on the hills that appeared far beyond them. Phyllis began to talk, as if the wide, open space they moved over had reassured her. She was going for the second time to lose a child. Her children either were not born at all or died soon after their birth. She was cursed. She knew she was. A witch had cast a spell on her. That was why she lost all her children. And that was why, she looked and smiled at him, she had married him, a devil. The very faint mist they walked in made everything in the moonlight as unreal as the witches and devils she spoke to him about. It was her fate. You could not get away from what was there for you. No matter how you tried! She knew he was glad for what had happened even though he tried not to show it. He did not fool her. He was only pretending, but she knew he was glad. Wasn't he?

Peter, surprised by the direct question, did not answer. His arm seemed to be bearing all of her weight. He listened to the flow of her words. They were walking on grass now. The grass was wet. The hospital lights were ahead. Peter was relieved they were so close. Phyllis became silent and thoughtful.

Suddenly, she broke away from him and ran over the open lawn, laughing loudly. He was too surprised to move at once. Fractionally, she appeared on the floor of their sitting-room, eyes closed, and frothing at the mouth. Then he began to run after her. Her laughter filled the night. Every time she slipped away from his reaching arm, or ducked beneath it, her laughter burst forth. Her pregnancy did not seem to affect her movements. He had not imagined she could be so elusive. He slipped with her sudden turn on the wet grass, let go, lest she fall, of his slight hold on her dress, as she twisted, laughing still, to get away from him. Finally, perhaps because she was tired, but laughing still, she stopped and turned to wait for him.

"You thought it was true," she said, breathing heavily, "you wanted it to be true. I fooled you. I fooled you. How I fooled you!"

She was like a fairy gone mischievously mad in the moonlight.

"How you would want it to happen!"

She was a child who had successfully played a trick on its favourite adult.

"I fooled you. I fooled you."

Her face was red with the running and with the success of her dissimulation. Peter did not know what to do. And, feeling a bit of a fool, he was filled with admiration for her, with pity, and with anger. Suddenly a white jacketed figure appeared, coming from the hospital towards them. The moonlight glinted on the stethoscope he carried in his hand. Peter wondered if the medical student had seen himself and Phyllis running crazily over the grass; whether he had heard Phyllis's laughter. He wondered what the story would be this time; what would be the substance, half-truth, half-invention, of this latest addition to those stories already told – about Jeannine and himself, about him and the women in the village, about his drinking.

PAUL

The other day Doux-doux, whom I had not seen for many years, except once, at your mother's funeral, came to see your father. After she had spent some time alone with him, she came and spoke to me. She said she had not wished to come. She had heard about the stroke and was afraid of what she would see. Your father, she said, speaking in patois, made her hurt. It was too bad. She spoke of God and his ways. Nobody ever thought that one day Mr. Breville, Mr. Breville, she repeated, would be like this. She crossed herself; spoke in whispers, and wiped away a tear now and then. She told me how all the people on that street had thought him rich. It was obvious to me that she had not disabused them. I could not help but think about her loyalty. Clearly, even now, she was impressed. She told me, speaking almost to herself, that our father had never set a foot in a rum-shop. Everybody respected him; everybody. She repeated the word with a fierce pride that her crying barely contained. It was as if she were talking about her father.

She said he had been the only married man on the block. His wife had been blessed by the Church and you and I the only children on that block who were baptized on a Sunday. It was obvious how special she considered that to have been. Everybody, she said, wiping away a tear, wanted him to be godfather to their child. And he accepted always. Even though he was always serious. I smiled at the understatement. She made him sound like a benefactor. But I had known his contempt for those whom he helped. I understood the gratitude that Doux-doux said they so deeply felt for him. He had been remote, had hardly listened to people's thanks, barely answered their greetings and, having to control his stammer, never spoken much. I saw how desirable he was as a godfather – representative in the Church of those who were forbidden to enter it to attend their children's baptisms because they were not married. He was an ideal representative. His remoteness, his stern-ness, like the sternness and remoteness of a priest, added to his importance among those whom he represented and despised, and earned for him the special respect that gratitude, unsolicited and unrequited but nevertheless expected, caused in the grateful. And it was a priest he most resembled. As Doux-doux so lovingly spoke about him, unaware of the contradictions, the stern black face of earlier years stood out clearly for me above the starched warder's uniform, the well-rolled puttees and the shining warder's boots I had so often seen my face reflected in. I wondered if she ever thought of questioning my loyalty.

Listening to her, I remembered our outings on Sunday afternoons when, replacing the tattered dress she wore during the week with a clean frock, but still bare-footed, she walked us along the wide pavement before the market. The gutters, since it was Sunday, flowed cleanly. But the smell of blood and offal still clung to improperly washed concrete. The other children dared not join us. Doux-doux, watchful and protective, drove them away, called them "ti-nègres sales". The young girl that she was then, whom I remember, made the prematurely old servant woman before me seem strangely unreal. There seemed no connection between that woman, still not out of her rags, middle-aged and experienced but uncomprehending, who had known and endured hardship and insecurity, who owned no home, had two children by two fathers, relied on God and his righteousness, and the young, laughing girl who stood at the corner of the pavement, hands on tattered hips, talking to her friends, and keeping an eye open for the approach of your father. No one could have illustrated more clearly what Patricia's mother had sought to escape from. She, too, had been a domestic servant. But her daughter had spoken of visits to her home by the people her mother washed for. They brought the wash now for her in cars. She no longer walked to their homes to collect it. Sometimes they came inside the house to exchange a word with her or leave a gift behind. All of this was a form of progress. Some of their gifts, and all the pictures, were displayed in the small drawing-room. No one else, on that street Patricia and her mother lived on, could display such pictures they had been given!

When I pass the mother on the street, I look through her angry disdain for my madness, which I know she believes deserved, at the clothes she wears that she could not have bought. Obviously, the gifts continue still. I think I see a quality of defiance in the way she strides along the street, disdaining the pavement, and if I see her early enough, I turn into another. I have lost my ability for confrontations. Walking down the street in the gifts of dresses she mourns her daughter in, she gives an impression of satisfaction at having stood on a principle and of having gained a victory.

I knew she was not sick that night when I entered the bedroom in which, lying on the bed and with a damp cloth over her forehead, she received me. The gloomy room, lit only by the small lamp sputtering before statuettes on a shelf; was filled with the scent of soft candle, nutmeg and fine salt which she had combined to make an ointment.

"Mr. Breville…"

Her voice was barely audible. It was even lower than the one with which she had asked me to come in after I had knocked on the front door. It was the first time that she had not called me Paul or Mr. Paul.

"Mr. Breville, you know why I called you?"

I said I did. She told me anyhow. She spoke in English. Nothing could have achieved less the seriousness she intended than those patois expressions which she transliterated for most of that meeting. I cannot blame her for trying artifice, by pretending she was sick, or for reaching for what she believed was dignity, by talking to me in English. I understand. I have tried both. She had summoned me to demand I marry her daughter and was not in a position to enforce her demand. She must have resented having to use subterfuge. But how else could she have authoritatively faced me? She was like a beggar forced to beg for something he imagined he owned and who neither owned nor understood what he was begging for.

She used at first a voice that was sickly and painful. Perhaps the pain was real. But each time that she called me Mr. Breville in that tone of cunning appeal and concealed resentment I despised her a little more. Poor woman! More than once I felt she would have liked to express firmness, authoritatively and without hysteria. And each time that I saw her control herself; thus allowing tacitly the weakness of her position, she made me feel, overwhelmingly as the meeting went on, the strength of my own. Yet I had not answered her summons with notions of strength or weakness. I had been unable to talk with your father about what had happened. I had hoped to be able to talk with her. It was not ultimatums, nor threats, that I had wanted to confront. I wanted to explain about Patsy and myself; to say that the two of us no longer had a relationship and to try to find some solution for the problem that her pregnancy had created for the two of us. Her mother understood my unwillingness to marry. But she had obviously considered marriage the only solution. It had always been the solution, no matter how badly it had nearly always worked, and when it was clear that I would not accept it, she began to lose control.

"What you think the neighbours will say, eh, Mr. Breville?"

"It's not their business."

I recognized the tone of my reply. It was insolent, and it contained the same resentment and opposition that your father, by his violent reaction, had provoked. I had realized that, once again, there would be no discussion, no opportunity to explain, no attempt to find together a solution for the problem that Patsy and I faced. That, once again, old, ready-made solutions were offered for me to reach out to. But I had seen them, those solutions. I knew that marriage to Patsy could not have worked, that I had to reject it. Her mother sat up.

"I not letting nobody make people laugh at me," she said.

I did not answer. Your father, too, had spoken of how much I had shamed him. And now I was to marry Patsy so that people should not laugh at her mother.

"If you think I letting you make people laugh at me… I giving you your last chance."

I saw what she threatened. I was afraid. I feared that everything I had been working for would crumble about me. But how could I marry Patsy because her mother threatened me? I knew her mother had never married. I said,

"Do what you want. I can't marry."

I felt resigned. I had had enough of tension and no longer cared. She dropped all pretence of being sick. Her subterfuge had not worked. Her dignity had only been a shell. She had tried to stand on it and it had crumbled. Her impotence alone prevailed. And her rage was the only thing left to assuage it with.

"Come here, come here," she shouted in patois, "where you?"

I realized she was calling to Patsy. I had wondered where Patsy was. It had seemed normal for her to be in the bedroom with me.

"Come and hear for yourself," her mother was shouting. She seemed not to care about the neighbours now. Patsy appeared and stood crying in the room next to me. She had come in from the yard. I knew now that she had been in the kitchen outside.

"You will marry her?" the mother asked.

I said no, I would not. I preferred not to remain silent. Even now, years later, I still believe that Patsy had never seriously considered we might be married. But I could not allow my silence to be misinterpreted by her mother. And it was for her sake, not Patsy's, that I had answered.

"I know what I have to do," the woman said.

I knew too. It was the only thing left for her to do. I turned and walked into the small drawing-room. It was crowded with chairs and tables. One was forced to move sideways between them. I stood for a while among the gifts of glasses stamped with trademarks, ashtrays with the names of imported cigarette brands embossed on them, and the pictures, of those for whom Patsy's mother worked, and of their sons and daughters, standing on the tables in their passe-partout frames. I heard Patsy's footsteps behind me. And her mother's voice, raised even higher by her rage, "Come back here. You don't have no shame."

I turned to where she was standing and said to her:
"Come and live with me. I'll rent a house."

It was a sudden and impulsive suggestion. But, and I can see that even more clearly now, it held out more hope for the survival of the two of us. Patsy hesitated. From the dim, ointment-smelling room her mother shouted,

"If you don't come back inside here now, don't never come back."

Patsy stood crying. Then she shook her head and disappeared into the room where the holy light sputtered before the statuettes and her mother's rage flamed. She had chosen. Yet she had spoken to me of her mother's brutality. On her face, on which, that Christmas day, I had seen trust and fear, there had been terror and confusion. Perhaps she remembered my own brutality and feared it even more. I went out of the front door and into the street.

PETER & PHYLLIS

The feel of broken glass remained. The bits were lodged between his gums and the soft lining of his mouth. He gargled once more and felt bits of glass move backward along the line of his gums to his throat. Quickly he spat out. One or two pieces of broken glass fell out with the water. But the remaining bits moved steadily towards the back of his mouth and to his throat. He awoke in a panic. Then, his eyes open now but the dream still vivid, he lay without moving. The feel of broken glass gave place to the antiseptic he had gargled with and to the memory of himself and Phyllis a few hours earlier. From the feeling in his throat he knew that the gargling had not helped and that he was getting a cold. He looked at his watch. It was nearly eleven fifteen. He had been asleep almost six hours. The door opened and Phyllis came into the room, the baby on her shoulder. She was smiling.

"We coming to see Daddy. Morning, Daddy."

While he slept, Peter remembered, costumed devils had chased him through the streets of the small town in which he and Phyllis had grown up, past houses he knew and did not recognize, and along a familiar road he had never seen before. The little town reverberated with the noise of drumming and the music of flutes and with the song of the masqueraded devils that chased him:

Give the devil a child to eat,
One, two, three children to eat.

At a corner, Peter, running, pursued by the child-eating devils, had seen Phyllis standing with her brothers.

"Say 'morning' to Daddy."

Peter, no longer running, looked at the retreating, green-ribboned back of the little girl that Phyllis had been. Phyllis sat on the edge of the bed.

"Go to Daddy."

She placed the child on his chest.

"I have a cold," Peter said.

"Guess who I dreamed last night," Phyllis said.

"I have a cold," Peter repeated. "Take the child away."

"My mother," Phyllis told him. "We were in the back room. It was so real."

Many times she had spoken to him about that back room, with the kerosene lamp instead of electricity, and of her mother sitting in it like a caretaker.

"She was really like a watchman," Phyllis had marvelled once.

Peter said now:

"I have a cold, Phyllis. Take the child away."

"It's too late. If she have to have a cold she have it already."

It was true, perhaps. And Peter, even though he was unwilling to expose to Phyllis the pleasure the child gave him, did not resist any longer. He held the child aloft at arms' length. It gurgled, hands and feet moving with pleasure.

"You know what she did this morning?" Phyllis asked.

Peter was throwing up the child and catching it. The child was laughing. Peter smiled at it.

"You know what she did ?"

The child was bursting with pleasure. Peter threw it up and caught it.

"You know?"

He knew, even without looking at her, that Phyllis was smiling. Never, when they were not quarrelling and fighting, had he looked, however fleetingly, upon her face, ever turned to his, without meeting the smile that seemed to be waiting on it for him.

"You don't know what she did?"

The child, in its intense pleasure, seemed to choke. Peter let it lie on top of him.

"She stood up," Phyllis said. "By herself. Alone. She was holding a chair."

She laughed. Her laughter was like a child's and, even now, still gave him pleasure. But the memory of their fights, and of the war without rules that they waged, surged, and he turned away from her to play again with the child. It was clambering over his body, falling back on to the mattress, getting up again, clambering over its father, heading towards Phyllis. She turned it around.

"Go to your Daddy."

She pointed to Peter.

"Daddy," she said, "Daddy..."

She seemed pushed by a necessity to make the child know and recognize him as though she were impatient and could not wait for it to learn to do so. Towards the end of her pregnancy, when they had been fighting more than ever, she had come repeatedly into his room where he lay drunk or becoming drunk, and sat on the bed next to him.

"Look."

She pointed to her swollen abdomen which moved.

"Feel it."

He drank, his eyes on the book he pretended he read. She took a hand and placed it on her abdomen. He let her; his eyes still on the book. There was movement.

"You feel it?"

He did not answer. There was movement again.

"There."

She seemed excited. He said nothing to her. And after a while she began to talk to him. He paid no attention.

After the child was born, she made him feed it. She placed it on the table when he ate, allowing him to have to remove its foot or its hand from his plate. And when he read in the study, she placed it on the desk next to him.

Peter lay on his back. The child turned again towards Phyllis and climbed on to her lap. Peter sat up and lit a cigarette.

"You don't have to smoke," Phyllis said, "you have a cold."

Peter smoked. She was like a faithful servant, blind with loyalty and protection. She would stick by him absolutely, in any emergency, any catastrophe, even those she might precipitate and which, more than once, she had come close to precipitating. In one of their fights she had taken up a knife as if to stab him. He had rushed to meet her, had slipped and fallen. And she had remained where she was, whimpering about what he did to her because he knew she had no place to go to, no place whatsoever, and waited for him to scramble up from the floor. It was only then that she had begun to brandish the knife again. She had held on to it for longer than he, who knew the pain the arm he twisted must cause her, had expected. And after he had forced her to drop it, she had pretended she struggled more and really wanted to get at it where it had fallen.

But it was more than a devoted and loyal servant he felt the need for. He smoked. Phyllis said:

"Although you know that smoking is not good…"

She shook her head.

"Well, well, well. When you get cancer, you'll see."

She smiled. Peter, on his back again, looked at the ceiling.

"I was telling you my dream," Phyllis began. And her voice, which he did not listen to, flowed on.

More and more, during the lulls in their fighting those sessions in his bedroom had become, she spoke to him about the past. She recalled nights when, as a little girl, she knelt on the rocking-chair that was her father's when he came to the house, and looked at the boys, Peter among them, sitting with her brothers on the doorstep. The sitting-room was in darkness. Her mother was in the back, sitting with her friends before the kerosene lamp, or waiting for them. Occasionally, no friends came. Then her mother sat the whole night alone at the dining-table until it was time to go to bed. Sometimes she worked – darned clothes or ironed. Or she read *True Confessions*, spelling out the words to herself and only occasionally sipping from the glass in front of her. Or she read painfully from her prayer book.

"I had never thought she was feeling herself lonely," Phyllis told him once. And Peter, who pretended he was not in the room with her, had pretended also that he was too preoccupied with the child to share her discovery.

The boys did not want her to hear what they talked about. They wanted her to move away from the window and told aloud stories of ghosts and coffins that terrified her. She had smiled telling him this.

"You all didn't know," she said. "It was the stories self

you were saying that made me stay. I was too afraid to go through the sitting-room."

But the street she looked at through the window was semi-lit. And many nights she had remained at the window, long after the boys had lowered their voices again and she could not hear what they said, because she had been afraid to cross the dark of the sitting-room to reach the security of her mother and the kerosene lamp.

Peter smoked, his eyes closed, a forearm thrown across them. Phyllis's voice, telling him her dream, seemed to blend with that other voice, hers too, which he remembered; and both pursued him dizzily down the abysmal darkness that, behind their lids, his closed eyes had conjured.

But when her father came, the boys went away. The steps were empty, the door and window closed. The children put on lights in all the rooms, and their mother, still in the back room, blew out the flame of the kerosene lamp and put it away. Her friends had left, going out through the yard as soon as they had recognized the sound of the car and the noise of the children running to meet their father. In the sitting-room, Phyllis sat on her father's knee. She sipped his drink, played with the long hairs on his legs. The boys were on the floor. Everyone was talking at once. Alone, in the back room, but under electric lights now, her mother was busy.

"The back room was hers. The front was for Daddy and us."

He could hear her voice relating her dream. He paid no attention to it. Out of the void behind his closed eyelids her voice, the one he remembered, seemed to come up again to him, tight with excitement as she recalled the times when her father visited the house.

There had been no darkness then. No one spoke of

ghosts. No one lowered his voice to keep secret what he had to say.

She had been afraid to go to no part of that illuminated house.

Peter smoked.

Her father's visits, she had told him, had made her father very special to her. She knew that her mother's friends went away as soon as he arrived, that the boys disappeared from the doorstep as soon as his car turned the corner. She knew why her mother's friends always called her "Miss Phyllis" and her brothers "Mr. Duncan" and "Mr. Lucas". Even after she had grown up and understood that they were illegitimate she had been glad she bore his name. Especially at school.

One day she and her brothers had returned from school to find her mother, surrounded by her friends, crying in the back room. And the following day, the day of the funeral, her mother, supported by her friends and dressed, like the children, in mourning, had stood behind the nearly closed jalousies in the sitting-room to look, as they had looked at numerous funeral processions of people Phyllis had not known, at the funeral of the dead man, her father, and at the legitimate relatives who followed immediately behind the hearse. Phyllis had explained to him:

"They had sent a letter in the morning to say we mustn't come to the funeral because they didn't want no scandal."

Her mother had not dared even to go to the church. Tearfully repeating the prayers after their mother, they had heard the bells toll. It had been a First Class funeral. All the big people of the town, black and white, had attended.

Still relating her dream, Phyllis was talking, in the

bedroom, about devils and evil spirits. Peter opened his eyes and put out the cigarette stub. Immediately, still relating her dream, Phyllis released the child, pointing it towards him. He lifted it and placed it within the enclosure formed on the bed by his body and the wall the bed rested against. The child was shut in within it. He looked at the child. Phyllis's voice continued, telling of the devils she had dreamed of.

"Daddy was different," he remembered her telling him once, "different from *maman*. You think he would ever do what *maman* did? Not Daddy. Never."

She was talking of the time just before she and Peter were married. Her father had long died. Her brothers had already fled the island. She lived with her mother in the now dilapidated house with the falling supports and the dancing downstairs every Saturday night. The partition between the back room and the sitting-room had been broken down to make more room for dancing. Her mother was up until all hours of the night. On mornings, Phyllis saw her standing in her nightgown on the sagging floor as though she never slept. Upstairs, at the back of the house, were the rooms for the prostitutes and the white sailors who accompanied them.

Phyllis was pregnant. Her mother, face twisted with rage and shouting obscenities, had called Phyllis all sorts of names. She had threatened to throw Phyllis out of the dilapidated house, "as if," Phyllis had said, "I was a leper". Only when she knew that Peter and Phyllis were to be married had the violent verbal abuse ceased.

The child was crawling over the restricted area on the bed trying, unsuccessfully, now that Peter was lying on his side, his back to Phyllis, to clamber over him. After a few attempts it sat down and began to cry. Laughing, Peter took it up. Phyllis had not stopped telling her dream. He put the child down again. It crawled to the varnished bedhead and tried to stand up. It put a foot on his face, slipped, and would have fallen. But he caught it and held it aloft with both hands, listening to its cries of pleasure, then set it down again in the confining space his body made for it. This time he lay on his back. Phyllis had stopped talking. Her dream, he realized in the sudden silence, was finished.

"You want some coffee now?"

The child was clambering successfully over the barrier of his body and it was pleasurable to feel its weight.

"I know you won't eat…"

"You're here now, anyhow," Peter said to the child.

Phyllis went out and returned with some coffee. She set it down on the small table next to the bed. Immediately the child, attracted by the steam, headed towards it.

"Take her," Peter said.

"You, give her to me," Phyllis said, smiling.

Peter left the bed and went to the toilet. Going past the bedroom that had been theirs, his and Phyllis's, and where, now, she slept alone with the child, he saw a part of her dresser and a fraction of his passing face behind the half-open door. In front of the mirror was a picture of himself in academic robes. The sense of futility and irrelevance it evoked remained with him even after he had bathed and was sitting in the sitting-room with a cup of coffee and a cigarette, and looking at the picture he had cut out from a magazine and pasted on the wall – of a soldier killed in action and lying next to his severed head like a fowl. Phyllis came and put the child on the floor at his feet. Peter watched it. He wondered what was in store for it. He watched its nyloned bottom disappear into the kitchen from which Phyllis's voice came to him.

"I'm making light lunch for you," it said.

PAUL

I know now that it is only we, the serious, uncertain masqueraders, fearful of the laughter of those who observe us, who commit excesses. Eager to convince, we intensify our posturing until the impersonation we intended as reality for others begins to assume reality for us. We play less and less for those who watch us and, in the end, it is ourselves only that we fool. It is then that, more than ever, we need to continue to perform. Otherwise our world ends. For we have become both actor and audience and to end our performance is to remove the need for both and annihilate ourselves. When I confronted Patsy's mother in that dimly-lit bedroom and the scent of soft candle and nutmeg, I forced her to question the role that she played. I replaced her as audience and she had been unable to persuade or explain to me. Or herself. The people she washed for, whose discarded clothes she wore, had always been able to arrange a marriage. I made her, who wore their cast-off clothes, see herself as the cast-off version that she really was of those who had worn them before her.

Months later, when I decided to become mad, it was to preserve my identity whole for myself that I reflected its bits for others to look upon. It was to preserve myself whole, too, that I had turned to Patsy among the embossed ashtrays and the glasses stamped with trademarks, and asked her to come and live with me. In reality, I was not prepared for so extreme a solution. I was young. I had strong social aspirations. I was a Roman Catholic like nearly everyone else in the small town. The future, for which I had more than waited, seemed close at hand. I was unwilling to jeopardize it. I knew, was certain, that marriage to Patsy could not work for either of us. But I knew, too, the destruction her mother had threatened. I temporized. I groped instinctively for something no man in my position, with my aspirations, had dared to try before. I like to think I had been bold. I know I had only been afraid and wished to compromise. When, crying, Patsy chose to return to the woman in the other room, who, she said, had been so brutal to her, I felt vindicated. And relieved.

But if I had acted instinctively, and out of fear for what might happen to me in a future I had worked for and wished to preserve, I had also, I know now, been reacting, equally fearfully, to what I had observed in the small town and shrunk away from. Patsy's mother, who boasted that after Patsy's father (the Indian who had not married her) she had never known another man and never would – Patsy's mother was not the only unmarried mother shamed and dehumanized by a white clergy into giving up her life to the church in a perpetual and unnatural expiation. And, even before the example of your marriage to Phyllis, I had seen too many marriages, forced like yours, that had not worked. I do not wish to talk about Phyllis and yourself. I know, and you know, how human you have been. It was from your example, which I had observed in scores of marriages before your own, that I had turned away that night. And perhaps it was from her own that Patsy's mother had sought to turn away by insisting as she did on marriage for her daughter.

If, in her confusion, she had resorted to subterfuge and pretence and been driven to rage when these had failed, I, in my own, turned away from what I knew and feared towards what I feared but did not really know. And, almost, I became what your father had been before me – a pioneer. Patsy, returning to her mother in that dimly-lit and sickly-scented room saved me the trouble of having to be one.

I know I should have been much more cruel to Patsy if I had married her. I have said before that she had no part to play in my life as I saw it in the future. Your father understood. At no time during his angry explosion did he suggest I marry her. But it was the only thing he could suggest; he could not tell me not to marry. So he attacked me for my "monumental stupidity". He was contemptuous that I had not been, like him, sufficiently careful about what the public knew concerning me. It was not a question of morals. I had been stupid, not immoral. Clearly, he approved my decision not to marry Patsy. But he found it difficult to accept what had made a decision about marriage to her necessary and to live with the consequences after I had made it. When I lost my job and could not get another, the financially precarious nature of our existence which, once again, he had to attend to alone, made him even more furious.

But Patsy's mother had had her revenge for what I had done to her in her bedroom that night. She had done what she had to do. The Headmaster had not dismissed me at once and on principle. He offered me the alternative of marriage and keeping my job. It was another ultimatum. I was surprised and outraged. I could not understand his lack of principle. Nor his expediency. I knew how understaffed the college was. Like my father, this white religious man who, with the priests and the nuns, had assumed responsibility for the moral tone of much of the island, was less concerned with morals than with expediency. I could not accept that a marriage afterwards could nullify the sin of fornication that had preceded it. So it was obvious to me that the marriage itself was the punishment. And that, clearly, had to be absurd. Logically, since it was a question of sin and punishment, I should have been fired on the spot. And that I would have accepted. But Brother C—, who knew us well, understood that I could not afford to lose my job. He knew how poor we really were. I saw his offer less as an attempt to be helpful than an attempt to capitalize on our need.

Of Patsy at that meeting I have no memory that is clear. For in that split-second when, seeing her sitting next to her mother, I understood why the Headmaster had called me to his office from class, she had acquired the nature of enemy. You know what happened. I refused again to marry. I lost my job. Patsy continued to live with her mother. Between the time of my offer, which she refused, to come and live with me, and that of her death, I never spoke to her.

And so, having lost my job, I set out, equipped with my academic and sports records, and my certificates, in search of another. I tried the Civil Service. The Chief Secretary received me for an interview. I knew him well by sight. He was a Roman Catholic from another island. Every morning, on my way to school, I had seen him driving himself and his family back home from Mass. I waited for some time while he wrote. Behind him, his jacket hung from a hanger on the partition. Finally he raised his head and looked at me. I greeted him and smiled. He did not return my smile. And as the interview proceeded, I felt, increasingly, that he resented me for something I had done. He offered me a job. It was a job I knew I could easily have secured two years before. He said it was the only vacancy. I mentioned my last examination and the quality of my results. He said there was nothing he could do. I refused the job and rose to leave. He told me that what I was about to do would severely prejudice any possibility of a future appointment in the Service. I nodded. I was confident. I still believed that my records and my certificates spoke eloquently on my behalf. I left his office.

My confidence did not last. I understood how much, like Patsy's mother, I was impotent. Or was I merely arrogant – as I began to hear that I was? I turned down offers to work as a clerk in stores, or in offices above them. These jobs were not for me. They were for those who had not finished secondary school or had been unable to get to it. Before long there was nothing more for me to turn down. I felt I was being humiliated, blackmailed and punished. My records, academic and sporting, and all my certificates, told me that I deserved much more than the town seemed willing to offer me. My refusal to compromise angered your father. Needing financial help – we had bought a refrigerator while I was at work, remember? – he could not understand how I refused the offer of jobs I considered were unworthy of the qualifications I had obtained. And he said to me often at that time, "You want them to punish *me*?"

I understood finally. I remember the beatings your father had given us, you especially. The people we lived among had been impressed by, and had respected him more because of them. I saw that the whole town accepted the idea of sin, guilt and punishment. And that the church, before it forgave, always punished first. I began to understand the influence of that squat, ugly edifice

119

that crouched in the middle of the town. I gave in to it. I took my Daily Missal from the new, expensive bookshelf and went with it every morning to attend Mass. You had settled your business with Phyllis very quickly. You had married her and then left the island alone to study. I could imagine what you were getting into. But I realized that my example had left you no choice. In your place, or if I had known before what I know now, I should have done the same. It is only the strong, not the impotent, who can afford not to compromise.

I went to church every day for a year. Michael was born. Patsy left her mother to live by herself. I heard how she and her mother quarrelled, how thin and nervous Patsy had become. But I still saw her clearly as enemy and did not feel sorry for her. Your father and I had called a truce. I know he despised me for my meekness but we no longer said anything to each other. And your mother had little to say to me. She was pleased with my new humility and my intense piety.

I learnt all about the Mass. I looked forward to each one as to a new performance. I compared the gestures of the several officiating priests. I derived pleasure from a change of vestment I anticipated, the quality of voice of a priest I preferred to hear. First Class Requiem Masses, with the tolling of the heavy bell, the chanting from the choir and the candles flickering on either side of the commemorative bier, gave me much pleasure.

One day, after such a Mass, I remained in my pew – I had insisted on getting my own – out of deference to those who mourned, and allowed them to leave the church before me. While I waited, an acolyte returned to put out the candles on either side of the black-draped bier. He had discarded his acolyte's robes and was in shirt and pants. His presence in ordinary clothes before the altar, while the mourners were still leaving the church, jarred me. The faces of those I looked at seemed still to bear the pain of remembering the person whose death they mourned and whose soul they had prayed for. I got up and walked dissatisfiedly out of the church with the last of them.

Outside, they quickly formed a group. I followed them down the street. I could not reconcile the returned acolyte, his shirt nonchalantly over his pants, and the people in the group, dressed in black, white and purple, who walked so seriously, so solemnly ahead of me. Others, too, took their grief seriously. They gave up the pavement to the group and walked on the street. I walked behind them, thinking of the acolyte and the performance his return had wrecked for me. There was a stir among the group. Increasing its pace, it began to cross the street towards the opposite pavement. At the same time I heard and recognized the sounds of a crowd enjoying itself. And I saw, coming up the pavement towards me, J—, and the crowd that gleefully followed him and his friends. I waited for them.

Behind J—, even in spite of the crocus bag thrown over his head and shoulders, I recognized Black Bam. Two ropes were tied about the middle of his body. Greene, frail and with his long mulatto hair uncombed, pretended he was pulling on the rope he held as he walked ahead of Bam while Duval, bronzed and unshaven, holding on to his rope, pretended that he was restraining Bam from behind. Every now and then, under the crocus bag, Black Bam shook his head, snorted loudly and moved his arms, pretending he was the vicious cow that the others controlled with their ropes. Every time he did this the crowd roared. Ahead of them, the only one of the four to wear shoes, unsmiling, erect,

J— walked, bearing in his hand a cigarette can into which people were dropping coins. The procession, followed, even at that early hour, by a large crowd, went by. Then, on an impulse, I followed it. "*Chat-a-founga,*" J— intoned solemnly.

And the two other men, grinning and pretending they pulled hard on the ropes they held, added:

"*Quatre sous pour 'oir-le.*"

Every now and then Black Bam played his part of a dangerous cow checked by the ropes his grinning friends held. J—, shaking the can, looked often to see how much money he had collected. Suddenly he held up his hand. Everybody stopped. The crowd, which obviously knew what was to come, formed a circle. I joined it, my missal in my hand. First J— emptied the contents of the can into one of his pockets. Then he turned to his friends. Greene and Duval had entwined about their arms much of the ropes they held and were now quite close to Black Bam. J— approached him, intoned "*Chat-a-founga*" in a louder voice and pulled away the crocus bag to reveal Black Bam's face. The crowd went wild before the revelation. Bam shook himself, moved his arms, jumped up and down. Greene and Duval, playing out their ropes, moved out, one in front of, the other behind Bam. For a while they tugged this way and that as, grinning horribly now, Bam pretended he was charging into the crowd. Then J— put up a hand solemnly. The tugging ceased. Bam grew gradually calm. J— went up to him and ceremoniously replaced the crocus bag on his head and shoulders. Then he moved back to his position at the head of the procession, the empty cigarette can in his hand once more, intoned "*chat-a-founga*" solemnly and began to walk slowly forward. His friends and the crowd followed.

"*Chat-a-founga.*"

And his disciples responded, grinning:

"*Quatre sous pour 'oir-le.*"

The coins, once again, began to fall into the can.

It was neither funny nor original. We had all seen this before: J—'s strut, his frayed black suit, his down-at-heel shoes, his longish black hair, parted in the middle, and his husky voice intoning, without any concession to the island's patois or its spoken English, the words:

"*Chat-a-founga.*"

And yet everybody, myself included, laughed. As if his solemn, pompous dignity, his upright figure, the un-smiling black face, the not-so-white shirt with the black-ened collar, the tie he had not changed over the years and whose tight knot seemed never to have been undone, the crumpled trousers – as if all of this had become a conven-tion we accepted that triggered our unthinking, recogniz-ing laughter. And it was surprising how many people dropped coins into the can. Even those whom J— overtly despised, who wore no shoes, spoke only patois, walked in dirty vests and tattered shorts, who had no remembered respectability to bolster their apparel with, who slapped one another with glee and laughed broadly, even they, too, dropped their coins. And J— accepted them.

I watched.

College boys on their way to school, to whose group, once, he and I had belonged, dropped their coins; senior Civil Servants, deliberately approached, smiled and dropped their coins, were gruff and dropped their coins, pretended annoyance but dropped their coins. Junior Civil Servants laughed and made promises about pay-day. They offered cigarettes which were accepted. I looked on. My understanding seemed to increase with every coin that dropped, every cigarette offered and accepted, every promise made.

Not so long ago, on this very street, J—, working alone as he often did, had stopped me to ask for a coin. I had stalked by him angrily. He knew, like the rest of the town, that I had lost my job and had been unable to get another. His cynicism had angered me. But, looking at him and his friends now, I understood the extent of his contempt for all those whom he performed for. They, nor I, existed for him. Except as the occasional provider of a coin. That was all each one of us meant to him. I understood this perfectly as I watched him manipulate the crowd.

I watched. The coins continued to fall into the can he held. The silly production was making money for them. And then a policeman appeared, in serge jacket and trousers, black boots and white helmet. The form of his truncheon was outlined against his trousers. He dispersed the crowd, broke up the performance. Greene dropped his rope and sat down on the edge of the pavement. He grinned.

"All right, officer," he said.

Bam pulled off his hood and stood where he was, black and solid as a house, laughing sheepishly. Then he sat down next to Greene and said something to him in patois which was the only language he spoke. Duval, resting against the side of a house, wiped his mouth with a dirty hand. A little apart, standing absolutely erect, the can long disappeared, J— stood, unspeaking, his hands clasped behind him, his chin in the air.

I turned and walked back the way I had come following them. It seemed that I had glimpsed something and that what I had glimpsed concerned me intimately. It was as if I had come face to face with contempt suddenly and for the first time. I who thought I knew it so well. As if I had only just recognized it and understood its worth.

I felt that I, too, to survive, would need to be as contemptuous as J— had been. Was it then that I decided I should become mad? I do not know. But the next morning I did not go to church. Nor have I been since. They say I'm mad. I know it's only that I have chosen a way to live with my confusion and with the pain that results from my inability to resolve it.

Just like your father.

PHYLLIS

Jeannine and Peter left the river bed to which they had gone after the dance and drove in silence up the dusty road. Peter was driving slowly, as he always did when he was very drunk, his elbow jutting out of the window of the car. Jeannine had been uneasy and afraid in the river bed: they had been close enough to the campus for Phyllis to emerge from behind any one of the distorted shapes – of trees and low bush – that she had been looking at in the moonlight. But now, picked out by the headlights of the car, the trees and the bush were too natural to suggest either beauty or menace. She relaxed and closed her eyes. When she opened them again, the car had stopped and she was home.

"Good night, Peter."

She kissed him on the cheek. As she got out of the car, Phyllis, the child against her shoulder, appeared in the glare of the headlights.

"*Mon Dieu.*"

But Peter already had stumbled out of the car.

"Go upstairs and lock your door."

Phyllis came up to where Peter stood and looked silently at him for a long time. Then she went and sat in the back seat of the car. Peter sat down behind the wheel and drove off. Phyllis began to speak. Her voice was inflexionless and monotonous. It seemed to Peter that

Jeannine's perfume filled the car. Phyllis, repeating things she had told him many times before, spoke until he had parked the car beneath their house. He heard her suck her teeth scornfully and the familiar expression,

"You think I'm your dog."

Leaning over the veranda rail, he waited for her to open the door. After a while he followed her inside and sat down in the sitting-room. But before long she appeared again from the bedroom, this time without the child. His head snapped forward as she pushed it.

"Stop it."

"Make me."

His head snapped forward again.

"Is white skin you want."

He got up and moved away. She followed him. Her voice, inflected now by her anger, threw the familiar phrases at him.

"You think you can do what you like... You know I don't have no place to go to, no place at all... so you leaving me here alone, just like a cat..."

He sat down on the veranda. She stood before him on the steps leading up from the lawn. Out of her slippers, wet with dew, her legs moved upwards and disappeared beneath the hem of her dress. He listened to the interminable talk. Suddenly he went down the steps to the lawn, knowing she would follow him. But he said:

"Don't come."

She did not heed the warning, got into the car beside him. He pulled the starter. He drove with the same quiet as that with which he and Jeannine had driven up from the river bed. It was as if he was not deliberately choosing the road that led circularly downhill to the playing-fields. But he was. He stopped the car in the centre of the playing-fields.

Phyllis did not cry the first time she got up from the ground. She merely rushed again, almost joyfully, to grapple with him. When she got up for the second time she was whimpering but she still rushed at him eagerly. After he had knocked her down a third time, she did not get up and Peter had to lift her off the ground.

JEANNINE

It was almost five. Jeannine left the apartment and rushed down the steps to class. Two hours later, when class was over, she walked over to the Senior Common Room to eat. Then she walked home. Because of the moon that would rise later the street lights were off. But there were lights in all the buildings she walked past and there was a light, too, in her apartment. Perhaps Peter, unusually, had come? She moved a little more quickly and hastened up the concrete steps. The front room was empty.

"Peter?"

There was no answer. And there was no note. She looked again. No, no note. No doubt the light had been on all the time and she had not noticed it in the daylight. She put on a record then moved through the curtained doorway into the bedroom. Phyllis was there sitting on the edge of the bed. In one hand she held a stick…

PETER

His daughter's crying awakened him. He looked at his watch; it was one o'clock in the morning. For perhaps the tenth time he got up and went into his wife's bedroom to look for her. This time she was there, lying on her back on the bed, her feet on the floor. On her upturned face, mouth slightly open, there was neither fear nor desperation now. Not even the child, clambering over her body, had aroused her. Peter, for a second, became alarmed. Then he relaxed again; Phyllis was breathing. He took up the child and walked back with it to the sitting-room and the brandy he had bought after he had come from seeing Jeannine at the hospital. When the baby was quiet he put it on a cushion on the floor next to his chair. He was almost overwhelmed by a feeling of unreality. But the taste of the brandy was real enough. He poured himself another…

Much later he became aware that Phyllis was standing quietly just within the room. He looked at her. Her glance did not waver, was as uncommenting as if she had just awakened from a long, dreamless sleep. He turned away. But the silence between them, when there was so much to be said, seemed unnatural and he switched on the radio. He turned up the volume in order to awake the child so that Phyllis might be forced to take care of her.

The room was full of music from a popular record. The child awoke. Phyllis came and took it up and left the room. Peter was left alone in it with the picture of the dead soldier. Pop music swirled about the two of them.

Later, he looked up from his bare knees, his trousers about his ankles, to see Phyllis, the child at her breast, watching him from the doorway of the toilet. He looked down again at the scars on his knees – from the days when he played football – and waited for her to leave. Then, as she did not, he tore off a piece of paper and stood up from the toilet seat. Phyllis watched him. The baby suckled.

And then, at the sink and about to wash his hands, Peter saw his face. It was flabby. His hair had begun to recede. His teeth were stained with nicotine. Suddenly his reflection began to laugh, soundlessly, rocking before him, its eyes grave, half-closed. He and Jeannine had been to see an opera two days before. The performers, with their period costumes, their naturally black faces, and the abysmally mediocre quality of their performances – after those that Anna had dragged him to in the metropolis – had reminded him of a picture he once had seen, of slaves celebrating their independence, dressed up in the clothes of those who had enslaved them and who soberly watched them celebrate. Peter had the sense of an absurdity, of children gathering about them the adult clothes they wore and hobbling smilingly about in too-large shoes, pleased with themselves. He laughed. His eyes in the mirror were grave. A vein stood out on the neck in front of him. He stopped laughing to regain his breath, turned away from the mirror, and was surprised to see Phyllis watching him. He had forgotten her. He went past her out of the lavatory. He heard her footsteps begin to follow him and the sound of the baby suckling her breast.

ABOUT THE AUTHOR

Garth St Omer was born in Castries, St Lucia in 1931. During the earlier 1950s St. Omer was part of a group of artists in St Lucia including Roderick and Derek Walcott and the artist Dunstan St Omer. In 1956 Garth St Omer studied French and Spanish at UWI in Jamaica. During the 1960s he travelled widely, including years spent teaching in Ghana. His first publication, the novella, *Syrop*, appeared in 1964, followed by *A Room on the Hill* (1968), *Shades of Grey* (1968), *Nor Any Country* (1969) and *J—, Black Bam and the Masqueraders* in 1972. In the 1970s he moved to the USA, where he completed a doctoral thesis at Princeton University in 1975. Until his retirement as Emeritus Professor, he taught at the University of Santa Barbara in California. His previously unpublished novel, *Prisnms*, was published by Peepal Tree Press in 2015.

ALSO BY GARTH ST OMER

A Room on the Hill
ISBN: 9781845230937; pp. 162; pub. 2012; price: £8.99

A Room on the Hill is a devastating portrayal of an island society (much resembling St Lucia in the mid 1950s) suffocating in its smallness, its colonial hierarchies of race and class and firmly in the grip of a then reactionary Catholic church – which insisted, for instance, on different school uniforms for the children of the married and unmarried, and three grades of funeral. The novel focuses on a small circle of the educated middle class, whose response to colonial society ranges from acquiescence, finding cynical self-advantage in the new anti-colonial politics, suicidal despair and various shades of rebellion. Its astringent realism in questioning the direction of West Indian nationhood is finely balanced by metaphors of as yet untapped potential.

At the heart of the novel are two characters, John Lestrade, who feels trapped between his desire to lead an authentic life and his despair that this may be impossible on his island, and Anne-Marie D'aubain, who unremarked by the other characters, shows the possibility of a courageous existential revolt against the absurdity of circumstance.

First published in 1968, St Omer's novel is distinguished by its sensitivity to issues of gender, its elegant concision and, in its existential questioning, an intensive focus on the inner person. If the world it describes has gone, *A Room on the Hill* lives as a major attempt to bring modernity to the aesthetics of the Caribbean novel.

Shades of Grey
ISBN: 9781845230920; pp. 194; pub. 2013; price: £8.99

As Stephenson comes closer to his girl-friend Thea, with her easy talk of three generations in her family, he has to acknowledge that his past is a blank. He has never known his father, not lived with his mother, and cannot remember what his grandparents looked like. He knows, too, that his failure to come clean about a disreputable episode in his life threatens their relationship. *The Lights on the Hill*, the first of two interdependent short novels in *Shades of Grey*, is a moving and inward portrait of a man, blown along by circumstance, trying in his halting way to construct his own story.

Another Place, Another Time goes back to the character of Derek Charles, who appears as a returning islander in St Omer's first novel *A Room on the Hill*. Here, almost a decade earlier, St Omer explores the circumstances in which the scholarship boy makes the decision to separate himself from his family and friends and conclude that "He had no cause nor any country now other than himself." As in all St Omer's fiction, there is a sharp focus on the inequalities of gender, and a compassionate but unwavering judgement of the failings of his male characters.

Nor Any Country
ISBN: 9781845232291; pp. 126; pub. 2013; price: £8.99

Education has taken Peter Breville away from his native St Lucia for the past eight years. Now, appointed to a university post in Jamaica, he decides he must see his family on his way from England. There is his mother, whom he loves, his father with whom he has never got on, and his brother, with whom boyhood competition turned sour. And there is Phyllis, his wife, who, though he has not once contacted her since he left, has waited patiently for his return, determined to be a wife to him. Once a desirable catch for a black boy because of her light brownness, Phyllis is now divided from Peter through his access to education and metropolitan experience.

In the week he spends with his family and meeting old friends, he discovers a St Lucia that, in the early 1960s, is on the point of emerging into the modern capitalist world, but where the disparities between the new middle class and the impoverished black majority has become ever wider. In the midst of this, he must decide what he owes Phyllis.

Nor Any Country, first published in 1968, is a profound and elegantly written exploration of the complexities of individual moral choice and an acutely insightful study of a society in the process of change.

Prisnms

ISBN: 9781845232429; pp. 144; pub. 2015; price: £8.99

Eugene Coard is woken one morning by a phone call to report the murder of a former St Lucian friend. It throws him back to memories of their island days, and his complicated love life in London that made necessary his relocation to the USA. Thoughts about his friend's metamorphosis from middle-class "CB" to criminal, ghetto-dwelling "Red" provoke Eugene to review his own so far profitable transformations. But just how much of Eugene's story can we believe? His confessions reveal him as probably the most unreliable and devious narrator in Caribbean fiction; has he, as a writer and psychiatrist, been exploiting the confusions of race in the USA to his own advantage?

With nods to Ellison's *Invisible Man* and a witty inversion of Saul Bellow's *Sammler's Planet*, *Prisnms* is a dark comedy about the masks people wear in a racially divided society that anticipates the metafictions of a writer such as Percival Everett. In the shape-shifting figure of Eugene Coard, Garth St Omer has created a character whose admissions will bring the reader shocked and horrified delight. *Prisnms* was written in the 1980s but perhaps because it was so ahead of its time, not published until now.